COME, WATSON! QUICKLY!

Five Unseen Tales of Sherlock Holmes

Mysterious crimes baffle Scotland Yard once again
As shadowy culprits abound afoot in old-time London

Jack Grochot

TABLE OF CONTENTS

Other Works by Jack Grochot

"The Case of Vamberry the Wine Merchant"
Sherlock Holmes Mystery Magazine # 9

"The Case of the Tarleton Murders"
Sherlock Holmes Mystery Magazine #10

"The Peculiar Adventure of the Paradol Chamber"
Sherlock Holmes Mystery Magazine #11

"The Disappearance of the Vatican Emissary"
Sherlock Holmes Mystery Magazine #12

"The Shocking Affair of the Steamship *Friesland*"
Sherlock Holmes Mystery Magazine #13

"The Case of the Netherland-Sumatra Company"
The Sherlock Holmes Megapack
This e-book is published by Wildside Press, which also publishes the magazine, where more of the author's pastiches will appear in forthcoming issues.

This collection of stories is a work of historical fiction. Names, places, characters, and incidents are products of the imagination and are used fictitiously in order to further the plot in each story.

Publisher: 221B Baker Street Press, LLC
Editor: Norma Itani
Cover Design: Thomas Gianni
Interior sketches by: Josh Grochot
Photography by: Norma Itani
Clip art: © The Sherlock Holmes Museum, 221b Baker Street, London, England, <www.sherlock-holmes.co.uk.>

ISBN-13:   978-0-9904742-0-3
ISBN-10:   0990474208

www.221bbakerstreetpress.com

FURTHER REMINISCENCES
OF JOHN H. WATSON, M.D.

The intimate involvement I shared in the adventures of Sherlock Holmes resulted in my chronicling sixty of his escapades in the late Nineteenth Century and early Twentieth Century. Those writings covered seventeen of the twenty-three years Holmes was in practice as the empire's only consulting detective, as he liked to describe his professional status.

Dozens more adventures never were put before the public at the time - for security reasons, or due to a pledge of confidentiality, or because of the embarrassment that would attach to the publicity.

Now, though, the stories can be committed to print. The security reasons have long since died out, along with their dangerous repercussions. The confidential veil has been lifted by Holmes and by his clients so that his extraordinary methods and his singular deductive faculties can achieve further historical distinction. As for the embarrassment, the change of a name here, or a place there, will serve sufficiently to disguise the ashamed.

As an additional safeguard, however, I have placed the notes for these new adventures in my tin dispatch-box at Cox and Company bank at Charing Cross with instructions that they can be submitted to a publisher in manuscript form by a writer selected by my heirs.

- John H. Watson, M.D.

THE CASE OF VITTORIA MARCINI, THE CIRCUS BELLE

My friend and fellow-lodger at Baker Street, Sherlock Holmes, occupied the wicker basket-chair near the hearth in our sitting-room on a cold March evening, puffing away at his old Algerian briar-root, bent-billiard pipe and complaining about the absence of engenuity in Scotland Yard's approach to the Holbrook Bank embezzlement enigma.

"Now if Inspector Alec MacDonald, with his keen intelligence and youthful, ambitious nature, were handling the matter," said Holmes wistfully, "I would expect it to be wrapped up neatly in a tight package within a few days, not weeks like it has been. He'd lay a clever trap and fasten irons on a suspect before the culprit knew what was happening."

"Do you intend to step in and offer your services to the bank management?" I asked, my curiosity aroused by Holmes's disclosure that the loan officer recently purchased a costly diamond necklace for a comely female teller who has accompanied him to dinner and the theatre on occasion.

"As you might have surmised, I already stepped in, just in the nick of time to prevent the Yard from botching the affair entirely. I am focusing my attention on the extravagant employee and his sweetheart with the lavish taste for fine jewelry. I examined a sample of loan transactions and have determined that one out of five supposed recipients of the borrowed money is a fictitious name - the person does not exist. My prime suspect has converted the funds to his own use, undoubtedly with the assistance of the affectionate teller. I am merely waiting for the official police agents to confirm my findings and ascertain the extent of the fraud. It is taking them forever to complete a routine investigation."

"What might transpire if the miscreant learns you have discovered his scheme?" I wanted to know.

"He could flee the jurisdiction with his lover and live a life of leisure in another country," Holmes speculated, inhaling the smoke from his shag tobacco. "That is why I am on pins and needles to-night."

In the morning, during a light breakfast of rolled oats and coffee, Holmes seemed to forget the predicament at the bank and concentrated instead on a cryptic message he had received by post the preceding afternoon from his older brother, Mycroft, an operative in the British Home Office and a confidant of the Home Secretary. "Clear your calendar for Friday from one to four o'clock" (the message read), "because the circus from Rome is in London. Here are two admission tickets for you and Dr Watson. Make certain you arrive early, for you dare not miss the promenade of performers and animals. Take particular note of the beautiful Vittoria Marcini on the lead pachyderm. She is a splendid trapeze artist. I shall find you in the audience and explain myself further."

Sherlock Holmes took a sip of coffee and grinned. "When my boisterous brother has something up his sleeve," he remarked wryly, "his flair for the dramatic is usually a prelude to an adventure with international intrigue. And he never fails to drag me into it without the prospect of an attractive woman somewhere in the mix."

"I haven't seen a circus since I was a lad," I chimed in. "How thoughtful of Mycroft to include me in his invitation to rendezvous under the tent."

"Don't be too quick to attribute it to generosity, Watson," Holmes countered. "He likely plans for your involvement in some kind of caper he has drummed up for me."

On Friday at lunch-time, Holmes and I were aboard an Underground train heading for the City of London, carrying bags containing salami sandwiches and fruit that our landlady, Mrs Hudson, had packed for us to eat while we waited in the grandstand at ringside for the orchestra to strike up a lively march to start the procession of circus entertainers. When the music sounded, the ringmaster in a formal blue suit with long coattails burst through the rear flaps, followed by a half-dozen clowns with painted faces and outrageous costumes. They jumped nimbly into the crowd, handing red, green, and yellow balloons to excited, screaming children and pointing to the parade of elephants that stomped in next. Riding on the first was a lovely blonde in a tight-fitting, pink outfit that sparkled with sequins, which moved rhythmically back and forth as she waved to the cheering spectators. Her feet were clad in white slippers and her hair was done up in curls on the top of her head, with a tiara to accent her angelic countenance.

"She is an intelligence agent for the Italian government," came a coarse voice from behind and between us. Holmes and I turned simultaneously in our seats to see Mycroft's serious expression, his bulging grey eyes fixed on the object of his concern. "Vittoria Marcini is in town for a dual purpose," he explained in a hushed tone. "She is here to enthrall these people, but also to deliver a message of strategic importance to her country."

"A message about what, and to whom?" the consulting detective inquired.

"That is the information the Secretary wants you to determine," the older brother retorted. "I shall give you more detail after the show. Enjoy!" he commanded, and departed, stepping gingerly down the bleachers on the narrow spaces between the onlookers.

For two hours, we watched in awe as the lion tamer defied death at arm's length from the teeth and jaws of the great beasts, as the elephant trainer guided his magnificent, dancing creatures with his hook and his gestures, as the tightrope walker crept across the arena without a safety net, and as Vittoria Marcini completed a double flip in the air into the outstretched hands of her trusted upside-down partner on the opposite trapeze, a fete which caused the audience to suck in a breath in unison, then hoot and applaud when the pair stood on the crossbar to finish with a flourish.

After their act, the audience dispersed, leaving Holmes and me at the refreshment stand with Mycroft, who had been sipping a hot cup of coffee on this chilly day until we emerged from the huge tent. "I witnessed her routine in Copenhagen and Berlin last month, and it is a thrill each time she does that double flip," Mycroft commented. "If she were not engaged in espionage, I would find a way to make her acquaintance and ask her to have dinner with me."

"Espionage? Tell me more," Sherlock Holmes begged.

"I thought that would pique your interest, dear brother," Mycroft said confidently. "Vittoria Marcini is working on behalf of Italy's ally, Germany, to wrest control of the Samoan islands in the South Pacific by supporting the rebels during a second civil war. Britain and its ally, America, are backing the ruling family with a naval blockade of the harbour at Apia. The British and the Americans have proposed negotiations to end the stalemate, but the Germans want to fight it out, to go to war.

"Our beautiful circus belle's mission is to disrupt any attempt at bargaining and to deliver instructions to a confederate in the British Home Office, a traitor whose identity is unknown to the Secretary. We are aware of this for certain because one of our own spies is privy to much of the secretive conniving among the Italian hierarchy."

"So, you want me to expose the betrayer and uncover the German plot," my friend sputtered.

"Precisely, Sherlock," Mycroft intoned. "Mother never did say you were slow to catch on. I have a stratagem that includes both you and Dr Watson."

"And why can't you deal with the problem using your own personnel?" Sherlock Holmes asked.

"Because we can't take the chance that the disloyal public servant will be taken into our confidence," Mycroft allowed. "No, Sherlock, the remedy to the situation lies in outside help. Your name was the first suggestion from the Secretary's lips."

"I am flattered, to be sure. What say you, Watson, to assisting the crown?" Sherlock Holmes queried, turning to me with a glare in his sharp and piercing eyes.

"I cannot refuse when my nation calls," I offered. "But I must say I would like to hear the details of Mycroft's intentions. What danger awaits us? Not that I am afraid of a little danger - I only wish to be as prepared as possible."

"Well, there is always the danger of being unmasked. No telling what the enemy might do to retaliate," Mycroft warned. "But I have taken precautions. However, there is no time to waste. Vittoria will probably make her initial move tonight, after the evening performance."

Mycroft meticulously explained his design to thwart Germany's efforts, and then he suggested we join him at the Diogenes Club for dinner. "I can answer any questions you might have over a plate of sautéed trout, the Friday specialty," he said expectantly. "We have plenty of time for that before the show begins again at seven o'clock. I'm famished."

Once our questions were resolved at Mycroft's haunt, Holmes and I were back in the grandstand a few minutes before seven o'clock, when suddenly a clown with a bulbous nose and frizzy purple hair appeared inside the rear flap, shouting in broken English: "Is there a doctor in the house? We need a doctor quickly!"

I rose instantly and made my way through the crowd to respond to the distress alarm. The clown saw me approaching and loudly informed me that a Mr Nicholi, the ringmaster, had collapsed just outside the entrance and was shivering. I found the man prostrate and advised the clown his leader was burning up with fever. "Get some men and carry him to his quarters," I instructed. "I shall examine him further once we're there." I followed them past the line of performers and animals, all ready to enter the tent behind the ringmaster.

Inside the ringmaster's covered wagon, the men lay the patient on his bed and hovered around me, as if assisting. "Wait outside, for what is ailing him could be contagious," I told them. They filed out, leaving me alone with Mr Nicholi.

"Was I convincing?" he pleaded.

"Absolutely, without a doubt," I contended, realising that Mycroft's plan was falling into place nicely, so far, and the taxpayer dollars were well spent on this charade. Now it was up to me to be persuasive. I leaned out the back of the wagon and asked the clown to summon the circus manager at once. He pointed to a gentleman in a business suit. "I am Thomas Claybaugh, the manager," the gentleman apprised me. "What is the matter with Mr Nicholi? Will he recover soon?"

I stepped down from the wagon and took Mr Claybaugh aside, declaring: "It is serious. Your ringmaster is in critical condition. The abrupt onset of the chills, the high fever, and the enlarged, painful lymph nodes are symptoms of the bubonic plague - a highly-infectious, deadly disease. Has the circus come from Bombay recently?"

"Only two months ago we were in Bombay," the manager apprised me. "What has that to do with Mr Nicholi?"

"There is an outbreak of the plague in Bombay," I alerted him. "I have no choice but to place the circus under quarantine, in the interest of the public health. You must cancel tonight's performance, send the spectators home, and have no contact with the London population until further notice - or until my diagnosis has been disputed by a higher authority."

"This is outrageous!" he blurted in reaction. "How will we acquire supplies? What will become of our schedule? We cannot absorb the loss of income that a quarantine will bring!"

"These are problems indeed, Mr Claybaugh, but the city cannot afford another epidemic of the Black Death. The quarantine is effective immediately," I insisted.

"If I tell you to go to hell with your quarantine, what can you do about it? I will not obey your order," Mr Claybaugh proclaimed.

"That leaves me with no alternative except to notify the police. They will enforce it," I argued, raising my voice.

"No police. No police," the manager asserted. "Many of my employees fear the police. Alright, you win."

"Good, it is settled, then," I added. "It is imperative that I obtain a serum from the nearest apothecary if Mr Nicholi is to be cured. I shall send my companion to fetch it. His name is Holmes and he is seated in the bleachers toward the middle of the grandstand. Announce that you want him to come forward, and then guide him here."

Mr Claybaugh did as directed and ushered Holmes to the back door of the wagon. From inside, I dictated instructions and wrote a prescription on the pad I always kept in my jacket pocket. Holmes scurried off with dispatch and disappeared into the sunset. Mr Claybaugh left to dismiss a disappointed, perturbed audience, and then to spread the word among the circus people that no one was to venture away from the premises.

It was not long before Holmes returned, toting a sack that contained a vial of what actually was apple cider vinegar, plus some syringes and needles. He showed the contents to Mr Claybaugh, who was stationed at the back door of the wagon, and called out to me. I took the sack, saying that Mr Nicholi's breathing was laboured. I remained inside with the door shut. "Oh, me - oh, my," I heard the manager moan to Holmes, who immediately struck up a conversation about the troubles that had befallen the circus.

"Dr Watson wants me to stand by the gate to stop anyone from entering or leaving," Holmes noted. "I'd best get to it."

Mr Claybaugh was left standing alone, but soon, one by one, performers and workers drifted toward the wagon, and the manager repeated for them his assessment of the situation. "It is very grave," he would always begin.

Around eleven o'clock, I opened the door and gave the onlookers some good news: "His breathing is normal and the fever has broken - the medicine is working its magic." There was a murmur and instant chatter. I saw Vittoria Marcini amongst the throng and wondered if Myroft had guessed wrong about her making an initial move.

As it turned out after I closed the door, she slipped off into the darkness for a rendezvous with her contact. She passed through the unattended gate and went on foot to a series of office buildings, where three cabs and horses stood waiting for fares. The circus belle gave an address to one of the drivers and climbed inside his hansom. As it departed, a shadowy male figure leapt onto the tail section, crouching and holding on for dear life with his fingertips on the ledge of the rear window. Sherlock Holmes was adhering to the script.

They traveled to Prince's Street on the banks of the great river, where the lady alighted from the vehicle and entered the lobby of the Thames Edge Hotel, which catered to sea-faring men at all hours of the day and night. She spoke briefly to the front desk clerk, who referred to the register and mouthed a few words. Then, Vittoria Marcini walked out of sight up the carpeted stairs - never to be seen alive again, except by her killer.

Holmes, through the glass door, watched her go and strolled

casually around the lobby, looking at photographs on the walls, to guarantee she was out of earshot before he approached the clerk to inquire about whose room Miss Marcini had requested. Holmes handed the clerk a sovereign and winked.

"It was a Mr Jones in 5-D," the clerk recalled with a puzzled look. "This is not a love triangle, is it? I don't want a disturbance."

"It is nothing like that, I assure you," Holmes laughed. "I am asking on behalf of the Queen."

"Humph!" the clerk grunted.

Holmes climbed the staircase to the fifth floor and found the door to room 5-D ajar. He pushed it open all the way and witnessed by the lamplight a shocking sight, the bloodied corpse of a middle-aged man stretched out, face up, on the bed, a dagger buried to the hilt in his chest. Behind the door lay the lifeless body of the talented trapeze artist, a cord from the drapes sunken deep into her throat.

Holmes rushed down the steps and accosted the clerk, telling him to go out on the street to roust a constable on patrol.

"Why? What's the matter?" the clerk sputtered.

"The man in 5-D has been murdered, as well as his female visitor!" Holmes exclaimed. "Is there a rear exit accessible from the fifth floor?"

"Yes, the fire escape," the clerk responded.

Holmes dashed out the front door and around to the back of the five-story structure to determine if he could see anyone in the vicinity. The alley was deserted, as were the two avenues that ran perpendicular to it. Holmes went up the fire escape, canvassing the entire dimly-lit area for traces the slayer might have left behind, but he found nothing.

When he reached room 5-D, two police officers were inside examining the bodies. "Who are you?" they asked together.

"I am Sherlock Holmes, the renowned consulting detective," he replied.

"Sure you are, mister," one of them spouted. "And I am Edward the Seventh, Prince of Wales."

At that moment, the desk clerk appeared in the doorway and bellowed: "Good lord, how awful!"

"Is this the man who came inquiring?" the other constable asked, pointing to Holmes.

"That's him! He killed them!"

"All we needed to know," the second constable ejaculated. "The guilty party has returned to the scene of the crime. Whatever your name is, mister, you are under arrest for the murder of your girlfriend and her partner in this affair."

"But I really am who I say I am," Holmes protested. "Send for Inspector Lestrade of Scotland Yard. He will verify my identity. The woman was not my girlfriend. She was with the circus and a spy for Italy. I have no idea who the man was, probably an official of the Home Office registered here under the name of Jones, surreptitiously meeting with Miss Marcini. I had her under surveillance as a special agent of the Home Secretary."

"What a story, mister," the first constable cackled in disbelief. "You can tell it in the lockup in the morning to Inspector Lestrade. I'll not get him out of bed at this hour for you to bother him with such a tale. Once you are a guest of the city in the Metropolitan Police Service hotel, we'll find out just who you might be." With that, he clasped a set of handcuffs on Holmes's bony wrists and the two officers escourted him downstairs, then into a paddy wagon.

* * *

"Well, well, well, Mr Holmes, what have you gotten yourself into this time?" a familiar voice chuckled at a few minutes past eight o'clock from outside the bars of the jail cell.

"Let me out of here, Inspector, before the evidence is oblitcrated," Holmes retorted. "The humour of the situation is growing old."

"The evidence, if there were much to hang your cap on, already has been collected," Lestrade said confidently. "Fingerprints on the weapon, that's all there was. Now what's this ridiculous business about spies and Home Office doings?"

Holmes explained the case to Lestrade as they walked to his desk, telling the official detective that Mycroft would be able to pin

14

a name on the male corpse.

"And who would gain from the deaths of those two?" Lestrade, incredulous, wanted to learn.

"At this juncture, it is as much a mystery to me as it is to you. But it is one I shall solve once I get my hands on the hotel night clerk," Holmes predicted.

"He has been interrogated thoroughly and still is convinced you are the one who did the deed," Lestrade grumbled. "I don't think he is hiding anything. But perhaps you believe you could be successful in squeezing more facts out of him."

"I shall confront him tonight and persuade him to come clean," Holmes promised, shaking a fist in the air.

"Oh, no, don't threaten him," Lestrade implored. "He is our only link to the events of last night, and I want him to have the impression we're friends."

"He obviously provided the perpetrator with the male victim's room number and is withholding data that is crucial to the investigation," Holmes lectured. "He is no friend to us unless he is forthcoming."

"Then pursue your cockamamie theory. What did you make of the crime scene?" Lestrade prodded.

"To some degree, I have formulated some ideas, but they are too premature to discuss," Holmes disclosed. "I can tell you this much, however. The motive appears to be politics."

"What on earth? Do you mean to imply that it is more than a common robbery of a well-dressed gentleman by a sailor down on his luck?" Lestrade cried out.

"If that were true, how would you account for the killing of the young woman?" Holmes shot back.

"It is as plain as the nose on your face," Lestrade debated. "She surprised the intruder and was executed because she could recognise him as the thief who stabbed her paramour."

"She surprised the killer for certain, but she was not romantically involved with the dead man. They were conspirators in a subversive plot. Send for my brother. He will set you straight," Holmes concluded.

"Your brother is a paranoid, too, but I shall have him brought here if only to mollify you with your outlandish assertions," Lestrade conceded.

Holmes returned to the shuttered circus, where he found me in the ringmaster's wagon talking to the manager, Mr Claybaugh, about the miraculous recovery the patient had made after his injection of serum. Holmes broke the news to Mr Claybaugh about Miss Marcini, and he reacted with utter panic. "She was the heart and soul of the show!" he yelled, sobbing. "This stop in London has been a nightmare! What will tomorrow bring?" He staggered out of the wagon, still weeping.

Holmes filled me in on the details after Mr Claybaugh left, and I guffawed at the picture he painted of his having spent the night in custody with inebriated prisoners and hooligans. We decided to take the Underground home so he could catch up on his rest and rehearse his important altercation with the hotel clerk that evening.

With a few hours of sleep and a succulent broiled chicken dinner under his belt - a meal Mrs Hudson prepared with buttered peas and mashed potatoes, smothered by her special gravy - Holmes invited me to accompany him to the Thames Edge Hotel to witness first-hand his encounter with the desk clerk. "I anticipate his reaction to seeing me out of jail will not be subtle," Holmes quipped. "That could work to my advantage."

We rode the train and a cab to the Prince's Street establishment, entered the lobby side-by-side and stood at the front desk before the clerk looked around from his task of sorting messages into little cubicles labeled with room numbers.

"Good G-God, it's you!" he stammered.

"It is I, Sherlock Holmes, a free man, and this is my associate, Dr Watson, who takes notes of my conversations," came the response.

"W-Why are you here again?" the clerk demanded sheepishly.

"I am working with the police to solve the murders. What is your name, by the way?" Holmes quizzed.

"It's Harry. Harry Black," the clerk said nervously.

"Well, Harry Black, I know for a fact that you kept your mouth shut about Mr Jones's other visitor when the police questioned you last night," Holmes revealed. "Tell me all you can re-member about the man. How much did he give you for your si-lence?"

"H-Half a c-crown," Black admitted.

"Go on, relay the whole story. He was American, I pre-sume," Holmes prompted.

"He was A-American, from the way he talked, his accent," Black acknowledged. "He didn't know the name our dearly-depart-ed guest used to register, but he gave me a description of him that was unmistakable. I told him the room number and he gave me the money, ordering me to act like I had never seen him here. Then he went upstairs about three or four minutes ahead of the poor young lady."

"That man is a fugitive from justice, the real killer, and you have been concealing information about him from the police," Holmes said firmly. "That makes you an accomplice. Redeem yourself and give me all the particulars about his appearance."

"Oh, lord, am I in trouble?" Black wondered.

"You will be if you don't fully cooperate with me and the police when they come back," Holmes cautioned.

"To be quite honest with you, he was extra-ordinary," Black went on. "He had long white hair tied in a pony-tail, pock marks on his cheeks, a brown handlebar mustache and goatee, crooked front teeth, icy green eyes, and dark bushy eyebrows."

"Excellent! About how old was he and what was he wear-ing?" Holmes continued.

"He was not old enough to have such white hair, about thirty-five, I would guess," Black said additionally. "He had on a red-and-blue checkered spring jacket, buttoned to the neck, khaki trousers, square-toed brown boots, and, oh, yes, I almost forgot, he wore a tattoo of a cobra with its fangs exposed on the back of his left hand. The decoration was recent, though, because the hand was puffy and red."

"With such distinguishing characteristics, he should stand out in a crowd, to be sure, unless he was in disguise, as I conjecture he might have been," Holmes observed. "Nonetheless, this will be more than helpful to the authorities. If you tell them what you have told me, it is likely they won't press charges against you."

"That is a relief. I beg you to put in a good word for me with them," Black said humbly to finish the palaver.

On the way out, I asked Holmes how in the world he deduced the suspect was an American, to which he answered:

"Come now, Watson, use your intellect. It was the only nationality that made sense, assuming my theory was correct. And, by Jove, it is!" He did not elabourate.

We walked swiftly to a cab parked a block away, rode it to the Underground station, and took the train to the stop near New Scotland Yard headquarters, where Holmes enticed the receptionist to send for Inspector Lestrade at his home because there was an urgent development in the murder investigation.

"Your news had better be shattering, or he will have my head for disturbing his sleep," the receptionist contended. "But because it is you who wants him here, Mr Holmes, I'll send a constable to notify him right away."

About a half hour later, Lestrade entered the lobby and uttered "Eureka!" when Holmes relayed the content of Black's interview. "I'll command that two men go to the hotel and take a written statement tonight," Lestrade remarked with excitement in his voice. "The killer is undoubtedly a stevedore or a deckhand on one of the ships in the harbour. My squad will canvas the waterfront in the morning and bring him in before lunch."

"It won't be that simple, Inspector, because the individual we want is not a worker on the docks or on board a ship - he is a professional assassin, a spy for the United States military."

"Here you are again with your imaginary cloak-and-dagger escapades," said Lestrade irritably. "You should be writing novels instcad of chasing after criminals. Your brother Mycroft came to my office today with a similar notion, but I sent him on his way, too, after he identified the male cadaver in the morgue."

"You have a penchant toward ignoring the significant, Lestrade," Holmes berated, "and an inclination toward emphasizing the immaterial. I shall find your killer in a place you consider unlikely, despite your intransigence."

"Do what you think you must, but read about our capturing

the treacherous thief in the evening papers," Lestrade boasted.

"The inspector has a one-track mind, and not much of one at that," Holmes growled softly to me on our way out the door. "He should be in a uniform, pounding a beat in a quiet neighborhood."

Back at Baker Street, Holmes bathed and changed into his lavender dressing gown, then consulted his Index, an encyclopedia of crime and various other topics, but he located nothing in the volume that would lead him to the suspect. "There is mention in one of the reference books on the shelf," he apprised me, "that America employs a vast apparatus of secret agents, many acting as attaches of the United States embassies around the globe. These agents can infiltrate an adversary's spy network and learn about clandestine activities before the other country can achieve its objectives. I shall send a message to Mycroft by courier first thing in the morning to see if my industrious brother can weasel some intelligence about the murderer from counterparts in the American embassy here."

The following morning, having dispatched a lengthy communiqué to his brother, Holmes loaded his old and oily clay pipe, settling into an armchair to review his notes on tattoo marks, a study he had made several years earlier for an article he wrote in The Police Gazette. Suddenly, after a half hour, he shrieked: "Our killer likely has patronised a tattoo artist in Southwark named Hakim, who specialises in drawings of the dreadful hooded serpent. Come, Watson, let's pay him a visit to see if he knows anything about the American. We'll take the Underground to London Bridge Station and ride in a growler to Hakim's parlour on this wonderfully sunny, cool spring day. We can leave the windows open in our diggings so the pleasant fresh air can clear the lingering smoke, which will give Mrs Hudson a reason to whistle one of her happy tunes."

Hakim's tattoo shop was wedged between a butcher's and a hairdresser's in a cluster of two-story, red-brick buildings with painted signs on the doors or hanging above them. As we entered, a tiny bell over the door frame tinkled, and a black-and-white pussycat meowed, sprang from a chair, and scooted off into a back room through floor-length curtains that served as a partition between the living quarters and the working area. Soon, a stoop-shouldered elderly gentleman wearing a turban greeted us and gestured for one of us to sit in the chair the feline had abandoned.

Holmes introduced us to Hakim and explained our purpose. The proprietor smiled with horribly-stained teeth and said he remembered an American who wanted the back of his left hand tattooed, but the customer did not have long hair in the colour Holmes specified, nor a handlebar mustache and goatee.

"What did he look like, then?" Holmes wanted to know.

"My client was short and stocky, with a bald head on the top and a crown of sandy hair. He came to me about two weeks ago with a pocketful of money, and he paid me a half-crown extra for doing a fine job," Hakim recalled.

"Did he tell you what he did to support himself - serving in the military, perhaps?" Holmes asked.

"He was in the military service, in a position that required him to wear civilian clothes and travel extensively," Hakim answered. "He was a tourist in London, if I recollect accurately."

"Did he tell you he was assigned to an embassy, in Rome possibly?" Holmes went on.

"He was to report back to duty in Rome, I think," Hakim replied.

"Did he tell you where he found accommodations in London?" Holmes pursued.

"Yes, he was occupying the guest house of the American ambassador," Hakim disclosed. "He was proud to tell me this, to make himself seem important."

"Your memory is superb, Hakim. Here is another half-crown for sharing it with us," Holmes said in praise of the old man as we bade him farewell.

"One other thing," Hakim mentioned on our way out. "He was carrying a pistol in a shoulder holster - I saw it under his right arm when he leaned across the table."

"He is left-handed, then," Holmes proposed.

"I hope you find him. I despise the American army and the politicians who control it. They are aggressors," Hakim snarled.

Holmes and I boarded an Underground train again, and on the way back to our flat, he decided to make a stop at Whitehall to approach Inspector Lestrade at Scotland Yard. "I need to determine something that will put the final nail in the American's coffin," Holmes confided to me. "The dagger that was thrust into the chest of the deputy secretary of the Home Office - whether it bore finger-prints from the left hand of the killer."

Lestrade, busily scribbling on paperwork at his desk, broke his concentration and answered Holmes's question with one of his own: "Yes, the fingerprints were made by the left hand, but what would possess you to ask?"

"A left-handed American spy with a snake tattoo is likely in Rome awaiting his next assignment - that is my only reason for asking," Holmes stated matter-of-factly. "Your search up and down the waterfront did not produce the anticipated result, I reckon."

"That is neither here nor there," Lestrade griped. "Tell me more about the American spy."

Holmes relayed the particulars of his latest inquiries and invited Lestrade to accompany us to Baker Street, where Mycroft was expected to announce the outcome of his foray into the United States embassy.

"For wont of something better to do, I shall go with you to hear your brother out," Lestrade agreed.

We gathered at home for afternoon tea when Mycroft's booming voice echoed up the stairs. "Sherlock, are you up there?" he called.

Holmes went to the top of the steps and motioned for him to join us.

"Have a cup of tea and tell us your news," said Sherlock Holmes when his brother's huge presence filled our doorway.

Mycroft poured some of the hot brew and sighed. "I'm sorry to inform you my contacts clammed up when I broached the subject of the murdered Brit," he apologised. "However, one of them want-ed to know why I would waste my time trying to solve the killing of an infidel. 'You would have hanged him in the end, anyway,' he postulated. How did the American personnel know he was a traitor, when the Home Secretary was completely in the dark, I demanded. 'We have our ways,' he allowed. That was all anyone spoke on the topic. I knew then from their virtual silence on the issue, their atti-tudes, and what little was said that the Americans were behind the mayhem."

"Still convinced the crime was rooted in a third-rate robbery, Inspector?" Sherlock Holmes shrieked.

"Well, now that I have had the benefit of evidence to the contrary, I am swaying toward your theory of covert machinations, gentlemen," Lestrade remarked reluctantly. "But if I take the American into custody, how can we avoid an international incident between allies? Why, we don't even know the suspect's name or whereabouts."

"Those two missing pieces shouldn't be insurmountable," Mycroft calculated. "I am confident I can obtain that data through diplomatic channels. As for the international aspect of the case, our prime minister is adept at dealing effectively with tricky repercussions."

"Then we'll proceed on your course if nothing else crops up to dissuade me from that path," Lestrade concurred.

After we adjourned, Holmes stretched out on the sofa with his violin, improvising a merry melody and soon snoozing, while I napped in an armchair with a refreshing breeze blowing against me from the sitting-room window. We were awakened by the ring of the doorbell downstairs and Mrs Hudson scrambling upstairs with a folded sheet of foolscap clutched in her fingers. "It was Peterson, the commissionaire, at my door with an urgent message for you, Mr Holmes, only one page, but very urgent," she repeated for emphasis. "Should I tell him to wait for a reply?"

Holmes read the note quickly and told Mrs Hudson that Peterson should not leave until a message destined for Inspector Lestrade was composed.

"Look here, Watson, the message Peterson brought to me is from Hakim," Holmes advised, and he handed me the paper to see the words myself. "I have new and startling information about the American (it read). Come alone to my place of business when it is dark, after nine o'clock. The parlour door will be locked, so knock four times."

"Watson, the game is afoot!" Holmes boomed. "There is just enough time for dinner at Simpson's. We can leave from the Strand after our meal and arrive for my appointment with the tattooist at the hour he dictated. And, Watson, bring your old service revolver."

Holmes hardly touched his plate at our favourite restaurant, picking at small bites of roast beef, potatoes, and carrots. I had barely finished eating when he urged we should go, and it was off to the Underground for another trip to Southwark.

"Stay here on the street corner and watch for a signal," Holmes instructed me when we reached the block where Hakim's shop was located.

"A signal from whom, and what will it be?" I blurted, dumbfounded.

"You will know it when you see it," Holmes reassured me.

He stood at the entrance and rapped four times on the wooden door, which opened momentarily, although I could see no one behind it.

Inside, Holmes greeted Hakim with a nod, and then a tall, lanky man with curly black hair stepped out from behind the curtains brandishing a handgun in his left hand, the back of which was marked by the image of a coiled cobra about to strike.

"You have been asking too many questions about a delicate matter, Mr Holmes," the gunman barked in an American accent.

Hakim interrupted. "May I present to you Mr Frank Eberly, my comrade," he clamoured. "He is not how I described him, because I purposely misled you."

"You told me other things about him, however," Holmes insisted.

"I told you things you already knew," Hakim corrected.

"You are expending valuable time on conversation that is worthless, Hakim," the assailant complained. "Step out the back door, Mr Holmes, you are going on a journey to Kingdom Come."

At that instant, the front door flew open with a crash, as Lestrade and three members of his squad burst into the room, armed to the teeth. I stood at their heels with my weapon cocked when Frank Eberly dropped his pistol on the bare floor and hollered: "Don't shoot! I claim diplomatic immunity!"

"We'll sort that out at police headquarters," Lestrade contended. "For the time being, consider yourselves under arrest."

"You are efficient and punctual, if nothing else, Inspector," Holmes gasped, then, turning to me:

"I didn't have the opportunity to send you a signal, Watson, but I assume Inspector Lestrade made a point of beckoning you to take part in the stakeout."

On the train in route to our apartment, I pressed Holmes to tell me what made him think Hakim was in league with the murderer of the British official and the circus belle.

"I made my deduction based on a drawing in the shop window advertising Hakim's trade," Holmes disclosed. "It was a depiction of the Stars and Stripes flapping in the wind. Anyone who despises America's aggression would never take pride in etching that flag on a customer's skin."

Some months later, the American was deported to his native land, disgraced and exposed as a secret agent, while Hakim was sentenced to five years imprisonment at Pentonville Penitentiary for conspiracy to abduct and terminate a British subject on special assignment for the Home Office.

The End

THE MORTAL TERROR OF
OLD ABRAHAMS

Sherlock Holmes stood motionless at one of the broad windows in our flat at Baker Street, breathing in the warm afternoon summer breeze and focusing on the slow-moving cab approaching our address. "We are about to have a visitor, Watson," he announced as the vehicle stopped at the front door. "It is an anxious, elderly gentleman who has spent much of his time indoors, judging from the palour of his complexion. I would hazard a guess that he has been in prison for many of his adult years. I wonder what brings him to me."

"Your assumption that he has been behind bars is a stretch of the imagination," I commented as I glanced out the window to watch our would-be guest ring the bell and gain entry via our landlady, Mrs Hudson. Soon she was climbing the stairs and knocking on our door, then poking her head inside. "A Mr Abrahams is downstairs waiting to see you, Mr Holmes," she advised. "He says he sent you a letter of introduction last week, telling you he would call today."

"Send him up at once, then, Mrs Hudson," Holmes replied, "and thank you for informing Dr Watson that I knew a little of the man's background before he arrived."

"So much for your brilliant deduction about Mr Abrahams spending years behind bars," I scoffed, while Holmes poured three cups of tea.

"Not behind bars - in front of them," he spouted. "Mr Abrahams is a retired guard at Newgate Penitentiary. Had I convinced you my brilliant deduction was genuine, it would have added to the mystique with which you surround me in your exaggerated writings."

Before long, a spry but worried-looking Morris Abrahams stood on the threshold, grasping his bowler and turning it nervously by the brim at his waist. "Mr Holmes?" he asked the two of us plaintively, and my fellow-lodger identified himself, then quickly faced me. "This is my friend and the author of numerous articles about our adventures together, Dr John H Watson. What you tell us is confidential and will not become public unless you give permission to Dr Watson."

"That reassures me, Mr Holmes, because there is something in my history that I wish to keep secret," Mr Abrahams disclosed.

"Your secret is safe, then," Holmes vowed. "So, sit down on the settee and drink this refreshing tea while you enlighten us with your story."

We turned the two armchairs toward him and Mr Abrahams began to relate his reason for seeking Holmes's help, his jittery hands making the cup and saucer clatter.

"I am terrified, Mr Holmes, terrified that an evil spirit is out to kill me," he said abruptly, taking a gulp of the hot brew and breaking into a sweat on his narrow forehead. "It is all because of what I have done in the past as part of my official duties. You see, Mr Holmes, besides guarding inmates, I was the hangman at Old Bailey, springing the trap door on more than four hundred condemned souls. I wore a hood so that no one in the crowds of witnesses would ever recognise me, but one of the dead knows who I am and has returned to Earth to exact revenge for his execution."

"What makes you think so?" Holmes wanted to know.

"It is like this," Mr Abrahams explained. "Last week, before I wrote to you, I was visiting my dear wife's grave at Nine Elms Cemetery, as I do every day, when what should I find suspended from a tree branch but a silk rope with a noose. It unnerved me no end, and when I reached home in Rotherhithe, there was another, dangling from the chandelier in my dining room.

"I interpret these events as a haunting from the ghost of a convict whose neck was stretched - a prediction of my impending death. I beg you, Mr Holmes, to please discover the identity of the condemned soul behind this malevolence and stop him before he succeeds in ending my life prior to my time."

"I empathise with you, Mr Abrahams, although I am not a believer in the supernatural. It is definitely a living person who is to blame. But rather than come to me, go instead to the official police," Holmes instructed. "It appears to be a matter for which the authorities are equipped."

"Yes, but they are cozy with the news hounds, and it wouldn't be long before my past was exposed for everyone in London to scrutinise," old Abrahams retorted. "If you handle my case, I am confident the deeds I wish to protect from notoriety will remain a closed subject."

"I see," said Holmes reluctantly. "Still, if I did unveil the culprit, Scotland Yard would inevitably become involved to determine if a crime had been committed, or if the suspect actually was attempting to murder you."

"I never thought of it that way, sir," Abrahams continued, "so what am I to do? I am in a horrible fix."

"You are for certain," Holmes agreed, "unless it is all a prank. Think about this strategy tonight - after a restful sleep, call on police headquarters tomorrow and discuss your predicament with Inspector Gregory. He is competent and imaginative, yet not a favourite of the reporters because of his introspection and reserve. Also, he can possibly arrange for you to be placed under surveillance so that no harm can come to you until the mystery is solved."

"After a restful sleep? Sleep is a condition that has been avoiding me, for fear of an intruder from the Great Beyond again breaking into my house, and this time doing me in," Abrahams complained. "But if you want me to appeal to Scotland Yard and talk to this Inspector Gregory, then that is what I'll do. I trust your judgment, Mr Holmes, because your reputation is what brought me to you in the first place."

"Good, then it is settled. Inspector Gregory will treat your concerns with discretion after you tell him I sent you to him," Holmes concluded.

Mr Abrahams took a long sip of the last of his tea, clamped his derby on his grey head, and left our quarters a little less agitated than when he entered. "He is afraid for good cause, Watson,"

Holmes observed, "because the hangman is a hated creature among elements of the population, especially since there were, I am sure, a number of innocent men in that array of more than four hundred condemned souls."

"Then why did you not concede to take the case?" I inquired.

"It failed to intrigue me - it was too commonplace, a routine puzzle within the limits of Scotland Yard's capabilities," Holmes contended. "Besides, I fully expect Mr Abrahams to return here, and when he does, he had best be prepared to confess the whole sorry truth of the matter."

"What? He wasn't honest with you?" I queried.

"Let's just say he omitted crucial data. If the walls of Newgate could talk, tales of private horrors would surface - and old Abrahams would be unmasked for the role he played in them," Holmes revealed. "Over time, I have engaged in conversations with five or six former inmates who alleged our Mr Abrahams was part and parcel to the disappearance of prisoners perceived to be misbehaving."

Holmes avoided mention of Mr Abrahams that evening and the next day, concentrating instead on an investigation into the Camberwell poisoning, a case that baffled Inspector Bradstreet and ultimately earned Holmes even more respect from the handful of Yarders who sought his assistance.

News of a development in the Abrahams situation came in a round-about way with an article in the evening *Echo* that described an eerie set of circumstances involving Central Criminal Court Judge Oliver Packard, known throughout London as The Hanging Judge because he sentenced men to death for offenses less than capital crimes. Indeed, he once ordered an impoverished defendant to the gallows for stealing food from a grocer, a friend of the judge who complained that the poor in the East End needed to be taught a lesson because they were robbing him blind.

The item in the newspaper depicted a distraught jurist who went home after a day on the bench to find a silk rope with a noose attached to the curtain rod in his parlour. There was a second in his bedroom that night when he retired. "This invasion into my domicile is the work of a madman who wishes to deter me from my solemn duties," Judge Packard told the police and the press. "When I learn who did this, I shall handle his case personally and deal with him appropriately."

But, alas, he never had the chance.

Judge Packard was found dead early in the morning, hanging by the neck from a limb of an oak tree on his front lawn in Upper Norwood. His hands were bound behind his back and his bare feet were tied together with drape cord, a washcloth stuffed in his mouth to silence him. He was wearing a striped nightgown, onto which had been pinned a crude sign that read: "Killer of Innocents." The judge, who lived alone, apparently struggled ferociously with his killer or killers, for the room in which he slept was in shambles.

These were the sordid, sketchy details Holmes gleaned from Inspector Gregory when he called that day to hear if Morris Abrahams had been more forthcoming in his approach to the consulting detective than to Scotland Yard.

"I am aware of the rumors regarding his participation in the disappearance of troublemakers at Newgate," the official divulged, "but Abrahams breathed not a word of it when he came to my desk and begged for protection. I am convinced there is a connection to the murder of Judge Packard."

Holmes informed the inspector that Mr Abrahams was tight-lipped and wondered why Judge Packard had not been under surveillance for his own safety.

"The judge was a fiercely independent sort and refused protective custody, saying he would not be bullied by a sneak and a scoundrel," Inspector Gregory stated. "He obviously miscalculated when he didn't take the threat seriously enough."

"Were there any injuries to the head, such as a knot from someone knocking him unconscious?" Holmes asked.

"None whatsoever. There were no signs of injury anywhere on the corpse," the inspector responded.

"Then we are dealing with more than one killer - a single assailant could not have accomplished the act alone," Holmes theorised. "Where do you propose to begin narrowing the list of suspects?"

"I could start with friends and relatives of the criminals

Judge Packard sentenced to death, and you, Mr Holmes, could assemble the names of inmates who disappeared, all classified as supposed escapees," the inspector suggested, smoothing his bushy, red mustache and pushing the wide front edge of his felt hat up to his hairline.

"That sounds like a reasonable strategy," Holmes offered. "Perhaps Mr Abrahams will cooperate, now that he no doubt realises his enemies are truly vengeful human beings and not the poltergeist he dreaded. But before I delve into the murky world of vanishing inmates, I should survey the scene where the judge met his violent end."

"We have covered that ground thoroughly and could find no clues, but you are welcome to try yourself," the official concurred. "Shall we meet at the railway terminus in Upper Norwood in, say, two hours?"

"That would leave sufficient daylight for me to accomplish what I intend," Holmes allowed, then turned abruptly to the bookshelf to examine the train schedule for the south as Inspector Gregory went out the doorway.

Before long, Holmes and I were walking toward the Underground station at Woolwich to board a coach that would deliver us to hilly Upper Norwood and our rendezvous with Inspector Gregory. During the ride, Holmes fidgeted in his seat, tapped the toes of his boots on the floor of the car, as if sounding the beat of a lively tune, and made comments about the gruesome reputation of The Hanging Judge. "He showed no mercy to anyone and would giggle as the felon was removed, shaking and howling, from the hushed courtroom," Holmes recalled. "I anticipated an assassination, or an attempt at such, ever since the day he declared he'd personally transform London into the safest city on the planet."

When we arrived at our destination, Inspector Gregory, his pudgy face and flabby frame obscured momentarily by the crowd on the platform, motioned for us to follow him to a carriage that would take us up the incline to leafy Hermitage Road and the two-story, red brick dwelling with a gabled roof once occupied by Judge Packard. The rope with the noose still swung on the limb as we proceeded along the walk to the front entrance, where Holmes paused to examine the pry marks around the broken latch. "The grass beneath the noose has been trampled by a herd of police, so the benefit of footprints has been destroyed," he growled to the inspector.

"Yes, but the earth is rock hard due to a lack of rain, leaving a slim possibility of any discernable track," the policeman replied. "I swear we have gone over the scene with a fine-tooth comb. You will not find any evidence we have missed."

Inspector Gregory led the way into the modestly-furnished parlour and up the staircase to the judge's bedroom, Holmes scanning the nearly-bare walls and the oak-plank floors in the downstairs areas through which we passed. "There was no disturbance here, meaning the murderous intruders carried Judge Packard, bound and gagged, from the second story to the tree outside," he surmised. "It is altogether possible there were more than two."

Once inside the bedroom, Holmes went immediately to the shattered pieces of mirror from the overturned dresser and examined each with his magnifying glass. "Halloa!" he shouted. "What is this? A spatter of blood. One of them has cut himself during the battle. I shall take this shard for analysis of the stain." He wrapped the jagged piece in his handkerchief and placed it carefully in his jacket pocket. "See there! A smudge of blood on the window sill." Holmes took his jack-knife and scraped the dried particles into a small envelope he produced from his shirt pocket. "Before long, we shall learn something about this miscreant that only he and his physician would know."

Not satisfied with that singular discovery, Holmes proceeded on his hands and knees, scouring the wooden floor and the braided, oval rug at the foot of the bed. "Aha!" he shouted again. "It seems someone has lost a piece of tooth. Here is a chip from an incisor. If it wasn't the judge, then this fragment must belong to one of the killers. From all indications, it was a ferocious fight." Holmes placed the evidence in another envelope and rose to his feet. "Minute traces of a killer's trail often provide the most powerful proof of guilt in court," he speculated. "Come, let's have a look in the rest of the house."

Inspector Gregory and I followed the consulting detective downstairs, which appeared to be undisturbed, except for Judge

Packard's study. Law reference books from the shelves were strewn about the room, as were contents from the desk drawers. "Odd that men bent on revenge would be searching for something," Holmes remarked as he examined their leavings. When he finished, he turned to the inspector and asked if the victim left any kin.

"There is a sister in Surrey, from whom he had been estranged for at least a decade," Inspector Gregory answered. "She is the only known relative, other than her two sons. They told me they were in their early teens when they last saw their uncle - and the sister, a widow, said she felt no sorrow for her brother's passing. 'He was wicked through and through, a sadistic tyrant, and the world is better off without him, as far as I'm concerned,' she claimed."

"What I was hoping to locate was a last will and testament, but there is no such document in the scattered papers," Holmes disclosed. "Curious, don't you think, that a gentleman learned in the law wouldn't prepare to depart this life unexpectedly and keep a bequest in an obvious place? Legally, without a will, the judge's sister stands to inherit his estate. We should harbour that tidbit in the backs of our heads after we determine from the judge's autopsy today if all his teeth were intact and what his blood type was."

Out on the walk, as we left Judge Packard's home, Holmes stopped to scrutinise the silk rope in the oak tree. "Not everyone knows how to tie a noose, but the murderers did a masterful job," he remarked. "Have your men canvass all the dry goods stores, Inspector, to identify anyone who purchased extraordinary lengths of silk rope in the last several weeks. There were five such hangman's devices crafted in all - two as a warning for old Abrahams and three meant for Judge Packard. If we learn who acquired perhaps as many as forty-five meters of silk rope, we shall guide ourselves onto the scent of the killers."

"I am one step ahead of you, Mr Holmes," Inspector Gregory said proudly. "My men already were making inquiries along those lines when we were investigating who might have left the warnings. So far, we have come up with nothing, but the task is not nearly complete."

"Excellent!" Holmes exclaimed. "I hope their search covers the countryside as well as the city."

"I told them to extend their field of inquiry to a radius of fifty kilometers from the centre of London," the inspector stated. "I'm certain that is an adequate distance."

"By all means," Holmes added. "Their efforts will likely bear fruit. In the meantime, Dr Watson and I can return to Baker Street, where I shall conduct my experiments on the samples of blood. Do send me a message there to satisfy my curiosity about the judge's teeth and blood type after you have received the results of the autopsy."

We rode down the steep incline to the railroad station in the inspector's conveyance and boarded the northbound train as darkness approached, disembarking at the Strand for a delicious dinner of pork chops and trimmings at our favourite restaurant, Simpson's. By the time we reached our apartment, the hour was late, but Holmes seated himself at the acid-stained, deal-top table to analyse the blood particles. He fiddled with beakers, vials, liquids, and the Bunsen lamp, while I caught up on the news in the *Globe*, reading aloud to Holmes the articles I assumed would interest him. He was fascinated by an item concerning a rival, Sidney Ward, who was credited with assisting the police in a case involving the robbery of a jeweler's clerk on his way to the bank to deposit the day's receipts. "If I know Sidney Ward, he probably was a conspirator in the heist - a more shady character would be difficult to find," Holmes conjectured. "I am intrigued to know exactly what assistance to the authorities he could have rendered. I shall make it a point to get the answer on my next visit to the Yard. But wait! I have achieved the result of my test." Holmes looked up from his microscope and motioned for me to take a gander, saying at the same time: "The blood lacks certain common antigens and is, therefore, type B Negative."

"This is rare," I concurred. "It is found in about five percent of the population."   "If the judge's blood type was different, as I suspect, then we have made substantial progress," Holmes proclaimed.

"Enough for one day," I interjected. "It is past midnight. We should retire and resume this project in the daylight after toast and coffee."

Holmes agreed, so we went to our bedrooms, but I could

hear him stirring as I drifted off into a deep slumber.

When I awoke in the morning, Holmes was dressed and preparing to leave for Rotherhithe to interview Morris Abrahams, this time to confront him with the knowledge of his clandestine history. "You can accompany me if you like, Watson, but, on second thought, I believe old Abrahams will be more candid if there are no witnesses to our conversation," Holmes postulated.

"I think you are correct," I responded. "I shall pass the time while you are gone perusing the medical journals I have been neglecting."

With that, Holmes crossed the threshold to the stairs, whistling a merry tune.

He was away many hours until, in mid-afternoon, I heard him ascending the steps, two at once. He rushed through the doorway, excited to tell me all about his adventure.

"Old Abrahams confessed to multiple murders!" he announced. "He was convinced he is next to die and wanted to clear his conscience. He and Judge Packard were engaged in a plot to rid Newgate Penitentiary of undesirables. Abrahams and two other guards dragged the troublemakers out of their bunks in the middle of the night and brought them before the judge, who would sit at the bench, in a rump session of court, practically in the dark, and condemn the inmates to death upon hearing the evidence of their bad conduct - no verdict from their peers, no appeal, only the ominous voice of Judge Packard in the shadows. After the sentence was imposed, Abrahams and the guards in league with him would escourt the convicts to the gallows and execute them secretly before sunrise. Their bodies would be interred in Potters Field just outside the walls of the institution."

"Good lord, a star-chamber inquisition! That is an outrage!" I interrupted. "How often did this happen?"

"On more than two dozen occasions!" Holmes ejaculated.

"What a scandal you have uncovered! How will the judicial system deal with it?" I desired to know.

"Delicately, more than likely. Information such as this could lead to riots in all the prisons and a demand for reforms by an inflamed public, not to mention the clamour in the press," Holmes predicted.

"No wonder Abrahams is afraid," I observed. "He just might be the next to die, if not at the hands of avengers, then officially and properly at the conclusion of a trial."

"Your presumption that justice will be served is premature," Holmes revealed. "I spoke with Inspector Gregory at Scotland Yard after my encounter with Morris Abrahams. The inspector went to his superiors upon my telling him the details and he came back to say no charges were contemplated. It seems the higher-ups were worried about the repercussions of an arrest and decided to disregard my report. Nonplussed, Inspector Gregory stroked his lion-like hair and beard, making the comment that old Abrahams and Judge Packard had performed a service to society by eliminating dangerous predators who some day would have been released to wreak havoc on their communities."

"The corruption worsens! It is widespread!" I cried out. "What do you intend to do about it, Holmes?"

"I made an appointment with Chief Justice Gilbert for the day after tomorrow," Holmes told me. "We'll see if he orders appropriate action. If not, then your chronicles of the case will expose the wrongdoing, Watson. The pen is mighty."

"But what of your pledge of confidentiality to Abrahams? He wished to keep his past shielded," I reminded.

"When he admitted his offenses, he waived my promise, saying he expected to be punished and anticipated the attendant publicity," Holmes assured me. "Not to change the subject altogether, but I learned some pertinent data during my chat with Inspector Gregory. Judge Packard's blood type was AB Positive, and his teeth were undamaged, meaning the killers left behind tiny incriminating signs of their identities. Also, a dry goods merchant across the Thames was burglarised a month ago and among the missing inventory was an entire spool of silk rope."

"So, you must solve the burglary to track down the killers," I proposed.

"Yes, and I know just where to start," said Holmes confidently, giving no indication of his plans.

That evening, wearing the uniform of a prison guard that

Inspector Gregory arranged to borrow, Holmes left our apartment after advising me he would return in the morning. "If all goes well tonight, my case will be nearly complete," he crowed as he scurried out the door.

Where he was destined I could not imagine, but the thought of a solution to the mystery kept me wondering until the wee hours, when I dropped off to sleep on the sofa with my notes of this episode spread over my chest. I awakened to the sound and aroma of percolating coffee, Holmes standing over me with a wide grin on his gaunt face.

"I pray that I didn't disturb you too early," he apologised, "but we have a long day ahead of us. Best we start it soon."

Still groggy, I rose to my feet and staggered to the coffee pot, pouring two cups of the freshly-made drink and seating myself at the table with my head in my hands. "Were you successful last night?" I asked finally.

"You might say so - I had a talk with one of the killers," Holmes boasted.

"Enlighten me, please!" I begged.

"He doesn't realise yet that I am onto his game," Holmes related, "because I want him to lead me to his accomplices."

"Tell me, in order, what procedures you took," I broke in. "For example, where did you go last night in your uniform?"

"To report for the late shift at Newgate Penitentiary, of course," Holmes went on. "That is where and when the two guards named by old Abrahams as his conspirators could be found. As a new hire, I was filled with questions, so I sought them out to give me the answers. I deduced that only those two guards, besides Abrahams, would be aware of Judge Packard's role in the conspiracy. Therefore, at least one of them was guilty of murder. When I spoke with the second of the pair, Thaddeus Pickering, I noticed a chip missing from his front tooth, a dead give-away. The piece I collected from the rug in the judge's bedroom will no doubt fit perfectly onto Pickering's tooth once he is in custody."

"And how will he lead you to one or more accomplices?" I inquired.

"He must be watched until we learn all of his associates,"

Holmes contended. "I already have left word for Inspector Gregory to organise a surveillance team. Meantime, I shall pay a visit to a barrister in Notting Hill who has stepped forward as the executor of the judge's estate."

Without regard for proper rest, Holmes went upstairs to shave and to change into his business attire while I enjoyed another cup of coffee. "Come along with your service revolver today, Watson, for there is no telling what crisis we might share," Holmes cautioned when he came back to the table.

"I would be remiss if I weren't prepared," I responded. "It will take me only a few minutes to clean myself up." I took a quick sponge bath and dressed in a flash, joining Holmes in the sitting-room when I was ready to leave.

We walked briskly to the Underground for the journey to Notting Hill and soon were waiting in the reception area of the attorney, Bertram Hathaway, who was in conference with a client when we arrived. Hathaway's secretary nodded and pointed the way into his office when Hathaway rang the bell on his desk after the client departed. The introductions aside, Holmes began by apprising the lawyer that a last will and testament of Judge Packard was absent among his effects.

"He always kept the original in his desk, in the bottom right drawer," Hathaway recollected. "I was his only friend and confidant, alone at the funeral except for the minister. The judge gave me a carbonated copy of the will, appointing me executor, when he wrote the text at about the time he terminated his relationship with his sister, Gloria Gibble. All his worldly possessions, including his considerable savings, was bequeathed to the orphanage of the neighbourhood church he attended every Sunday. He was very religious, despite his reputation as a callous authoritarian."

"You have answered all my questions even before I asked one," Holmes quipped. "You have been extremely helpful."

"I hope you get to the bottom of this with speed, Mr Holmes," Hathaway replied. "You see, Judge Packard was like a father to me. It was because of his guidance that I chose this profession. He sponsored my admission to the school of law and provided financial support each year I was there. Afterward, he gave me aid to establish this practice, never demanding anything in return, so I actually owed my career to him."

We bid the barrister adieu and traveled by train over the vast river to the quaint town of Guildford in Surrey, where Sherlock Holmes knew, from his dialogues with Inspector Gregory, that the widow Gibble made her home with her two grown sons. Holmes went directly to the headquarters of the local police, saying that if anyone was acquainted with the particulars about the family, it would be the constable who patrols the street on which they live.

"That would be Stanley Garfield," the desk sergeant signified, referring to a large, colour-coded map on the wall behind him. "You're in luck - he is due here for a lunch break in about ten minutes."

Garfield was prompt, standing erect before the sergeant to report all was quiet at the end of the morning rounds. He greeted Holmes and me with a polite and awe-struck attitude, admiring the depiction of our adventures in the magazines. "I have followed every word of your thrilling escapades and am quite impressed by your successes," he praised.

"You are not familiar, then, with the failures," Holmes humbly retorted. "Dr Watson seldom mentions them. Possibly you can assist me in one affair that might eventually be counted among the winners. I am interested in what intelligence you possess on the Gibbles of Endell Avenue."

"A sorry bunch, to be sure," Garfield replied. "The woman, Gloria, is extremely protective of her two boys, bad apples in my book. The older one, Errol, served a nine-month stretch in Newgate for burglary, and the younger one, Alex, dances to Errol's tune. When Errol is up to no good, Alex is always at his side. Right now they are my prime suspects in the robbery of a Wandsworth shopkeeper. The victim was pistol-whipped unmercifully by two masked gunmen who escaped with only about fifty pounds from the cash box."

"Now I must discern their blood types," Holmes continued. "Who and where is the town physician?"

"Old Dr Adams would know. He delivered both boys and has complained to me more than once that he was disappointed in the way they turned out," Garfield noted further, offering to quiz the town's elderly practitioner on behalf of Homes. "Doc Adams would speak more freely to me than to you, Mr Holmes, about confidential matters. What have the Gibble boys done, if you don't mind confiding in me?"

"I am investigating the murder of their uncle, Judge Packard," Holmes disclosed, "but I can't yet be certain of their involvement. That is why I need to learn their blood types - the killers left a small sample of blood in the judge's bedroom, and the blood type is rare."

"Well, those two ne'er-do-wells are capable of such a crime, to be sure. I usually pass the doctor's office around two o'clock. I'll meet you at the Henrietta Street Cafe about half-past the hour."

Holmes and I left Garfield eating a salami-and-onion sandwich in the squad room. We meandered through the business district, entering the cafe for a bowl of chicken noodle soup and a platter of fried, breaded drumsticks. After the satisfying meal, there was about an hour remaining until Garfield would arrive, so we ventured down the block to a tobacco store and bought a supply of our preferred smokes. We returned to the restaurant a little before two-thirty, waiting in a booth with cups of tea.

The constable spied us right away and made a bee-line to where we sat, sliding onto the bench beside Holmes. In a low voice, he spouted the results of his inquiry. "Doc Adams didn't even resort to his files - he knew the answer to my question off the top of his head: The brothers both have a rare blood type, B Negative, passed down from their late father's side of the family."

"That seals it, then," Holmes stated calmly. "It is the identical blood type I found at the scene. It is sufficient evidence to support a writ to search their household and the dwelling of Thaddeus Pickering, the Newgate guard I believe to be an accomplice in the judge's violent death."

"Thaddeus Pickering, no less - he has been one of Errol Gibble's associates ever since he was released from the penitentiary," Garfield chimed in.

"More evidence of their plotting," Holmes proclaimed. "You have been a valuable asset to my case, Constable Garfield. I shall give you proper credit when I unravel my findings at Scotland

Yard."

Inspector Gregory listened intently to Holmes's recital of the facts and grumbled that he should have focused on the Gibble brothers after Holmes noticed the last will and testament of Judge Packard was nowhere to be located in his residence.

"I'll obtain a writ today and we'll comb through their possessions. What exactly will we be looking for, Mr Holmes?"

"You will know it as soon as you see it, Inspector," Holmes cryptically answered.

It was supper time for the Gibbles when Gregory and two other inspectors knocked on the front door, and the mother came to the stoop, perturbed. "My sons are eating, you will have to come back," she growled. "Why are you policemen always hassling them? They have done nothing wrong."

"We are probing the killing of your brother, Gloria, and we believe they are to blame," Inspector Gregory informed her, then forced his way past her in the doorway, followed by the other two detectives, Holmes, and me.

"Help! Help! I am being attacked!" Mrs Gibble screamed, causing her sons to burst into the room with firearms. We all drew our revolvers and aimed them at the suspects, shouting "Police! Police!" The boys lowered their handguns and protested the intrusion, to which Inspector Gregory, still pointing his Webley in their direction, responded by ordering them to the settee. He directed Mrs Gibble to an armchair and instructed one of the inspectors to keep them under watch while the search was conducted.

"What do you coppers want to pin on us now?" Errol Gibble pleaded in a harsh tone.

"We'll talk after we've finished," Inspector Gregory replied, then turned to the three of us standing to the side and said we would start in the cellar and work our way up to the second floor. On the way down the narrow stairs, ducking our heads beneath the low ceiling, Inspector Gregory spoke to Holmes in a whisper: "It would be a help if I knew what we were after."

When we reached the dirt floor together, Holmes, holding an oil lamp, swept it across a wide area and beckoned the inspector to a corner that contained a small table and two wooden chairs.

On the tabletop, resting on end, was a large spool of silk rope, most of it gone.

"Eureka!" bellowed the inspector. "What better evidence could there be?"

"Perhaps this," offered Holmes, holding an open carpet bag in his free hand. Inside, we could see a section of the rope, a noose tied at the end. "Obviously, this was meant for Morris Abrahams, but your men protecting him deterred these reprobates from completing their grisly task," Holmes speculated. "Look here, under the rope! There is a note with a safety pin. 'Killer of Innocents,' it says."

"Just like the one fastened to the judge's nightgown. We have caught our murderers, like rats in a trap," Inspector Gregory howled.

"Not all of them, Inspector, there is another," Holmes reminded. "The evidence against Pickering is solid, but we need more if the Gibble brothers don't own up to their deed and finger him as a participant."

Getting the Gibbles to talk was a monumental hurdle Inspector Gregory and Holmes faced when we went back to the sitting-room.

"You coppers can take a flying leap off a cliff - I don't co-operate with the law," barked Errol. "And don't you say a thing, either, Alex, or I'll snuff you out before you can testify."

"Don't worry, big brother, my mouth is shut tight," said the younger one.

After they were handcuffed and led to a carriage for a ride to the local jail, Holmes and Inspector Gregory concocted their next move on the way to Scotland Yard. Holmes would report for duty again as an apprentice night guard at Newgate, startle Pickering with Holmes's true identity, brace the accomplice with the evidence against him, and persuade him to come clean. In return, Pickering would receive a life sentence instead of swinging on the gallows with his friends, the Gibbles. Part of the bargain to spare his life would be a stipulation that he corroborate the testimony of Morris Abrahams, who was destined to reveal in open court the conspiracy to hang troublesome convicts.

That night, Pickering was panic-stricken when Holmes accosted him. Hardened as he was, Pickering trembled and sank onto one knee, begging for leniency. Sobbing, he accepted the terms of the deal, confessing to Holmes that the revenge motive for the judge's killing, and the planned murder of old Abrahams, was all a ruse to throw off suspicion for the real reason: money. According to Pickering, the Gibble boys and he agreed to share the proceeds of the judge's estate - after the sons had poisoned their mother.

The End

THE DEADLY GOODGE STREET AFFAIR

Part 1
HEINOUS CRIMES AND THEIR AFTERMATH

Chapter 1
THE DECOYS AND THE DOUBLE-CROSS

Vincent Munroe, a man of violence and dishonesty, gathered his underlings in the cellar of his two-story, Tudor-style house on the outskirts of London to lay bare his plan for robbing the Farmers and Merchants Bank in the borough of Bromley on a day the Eureka Mining Company of New Zealand deposited its payroll. Munroe spoke in a hushed tone, as if the law were within earshot of a normal voice, chastising the gang members for talking among themselves when he had more important things to say. "Now pay attention, you blokes," he ordered, "because the timing of this little caper is crucial. We can't miss a step, or the coppers will descend upon us and wrap us in chains before the money, in the delivery sacks, pretty as you please, is handed over to us to haul away and divide here in this cozy nook Friday evening. If everything goes right, we can all live like kings for a long while and make donations to charity for the poor souls who have walked the straight and narrow."

Munroe took a long drag on his cigarette and began to explain his plan, issuing an assignment to each of the assembled hoodlums.

"And what is your job, Munroe?" asked one of them, Harry Hempfield, indignantly. "Where will you be while we are taking all the risks?" The group mumbled in agreement.

Munroe bristled at the implication that he would be safely off to the side of the danger: "I'll be seated at a bank clerk's desk, opening an account, to make certain nothing goes wrong, and to surprise whoever tries to kibosh the operation - surprise them with the revolver I always keep tucked in a holster under my waistcoat."

"You're the look-out, then, soft enough duty for the brains of the outfit," Hempfield countered angrily. "I'm fed up with doing all the dirty work. Why don't you let me be the look-out?"

"Because you don't have a brain smart enough for that," the leader argued. "That's the reason I'm in charge - I have more brain power than the lot of you put together," a comment that brought forth more mumbling from the miscreants. "So that's the plan, take it or leave it," Munroe barked. "You're either in or you're out."

"Count me in, boss," declared Sean O'Grady. "I'm with you one hundred percent."

"What about the rest of you?" Munroe demanded.

There was consensus to go along with Munroe's scheme, some members of the gang nodding and others offering a word or two of acquiescence.

"What about you, Hempfield, are you with us?" Munroe wanted to know.

"I guess so, yeah," the reluctant thief conceded.

"It's essential that you show some enthusiasm, Harry," Munroe continued, "because you and Wilson are key players in this game. You are the decoys who will create the diversion the rest of the crew needs to slip out of the bank unmolested."

"I'll do my part, but I'll curb the enthusiasm," Harry Hempfield concluded.

Munroe dismissed his band of criminals, instructing them to rendezvous at eight o'clock in the morning on Friday to review the plan and yet have plenty of time to reach their positions before the mining company money arrived at the bank on schedule, a pattern he had watched develop over the preceding three Fridays.

After the men had all gone off in various directions, until three days hence, Vincent Munroe sat in a creaky kitchen chair, drinking coffee and contemplating the near-insurrection in the cellar hideaway. "Intolerable," he said aloud to himself, finally deciding on the remedy for conduct that challenged his authority.

The mastermind of the impending brazen holdup set himself upon the task of constructing a bomb. He grinned broadly as he toiled delicately with two sticks of dynamite and a trigger mechanism he invented using wooden matches, a short, fast-burning fuse, a shard of flint, and a piece of metal attached to a pull-cord. The explosion would occur within ten seconds after the cord was jerked on the outside of a box that contained the dynamite and several hundred nails. Munroe had assured Harry Hempfield and Frederick Wilson, the two decoys, that they would have upwards of thirty seconds to exit the bakery, six doors up from the bank, before the blast went off. The deafening sound and ensuing conflagration would divert the attention of the two constables who routinely stationed themselves beside the wagon carrying the payroll shipment. Munroe's lie to Hempfield and Wilson about the timing would serve to eliminate two troublesome co-conspirators. The other recalcitrant subordinates would suffer similar fates during the robbery itself inside the Farmers and Merchants Bank, the merciless conniver reckoned with a sinister chuckle. And he dreamed with avarice about the wealth he no longer would be obliged to share with the malcontents.

Chapter 2
CONSTERNATION AND AN ESCAPE

On that ferocious and sadistic Friday in the spring of 1875, Vincent Munroe positioned his band of ne'er-do-wells in various locations within proximity to the Farmers and Merchants Bank, instructing them precisely when to move in and wreak havoc among the victims of his vicious scenario. Tall and wiry, the bandit chieftain leaned his bony shoulder against the hitching post near the entrance to the bank, crossed his legs, and puffed on an expensive cigar until he glimpsed the mining company wagon approaching from the north along the busy avenue. He took off his broad-brimmed hat and wiped his brow with a red handkerchief to signal his confederates that the moment for them to spring into action was at hand.

On board the wagon in the driver's seat were two men who would deliver the payroll, and in the bed, on wooden chairs, were two guards armed with sawed-off, twelve-gauge, double-barreled shotguns loaded with buckshot. The pair of bay horses pulling the wagon halted at the hitching post as Munroe made his way into the bank and stood casually at an account clerk's desk on the outside of an oak railing, which separated the pedestrian area from the section housing the vault and the teller compartments. The clerk looked up from the ledger he was reading, placed his pencil behind his ear, and asked how he could help the unfamiliar gentleman with his hands in his trouser pockets.

"My name is Arthur McDevitt, and I wish to open a savings account," Munroe advised.

"By all means, have this seat beside me and tell me how much cash you wish to deposit today," the unsuspecting clerk responded, smiling. As he spoke, the two mine company employees entered, each carrying two money bags and followed by the guards with their weapons in their right hands, pointing toward the floor. The clerk excused himself abruptly and rose to open the gate on the oak railing for all four to pass through to the vault.

As he did, the deafening noise of a horrendous explosion pierced the quiet of the morning in a neighboring building. Moments later, three hooded assailants burst through the front entrance to the bank, brandishing revolvers, while one of them shouted, "Robbery! Drop the shotguns! We have you covered! Get face down on the floor! Everyone!"

Startled and frightened, three customers and the clerk obeyed instantly, but the two guards raised their terrible weapons and opened fire, one of the blasts cutting Sean O'Grady in half at the abdomen, another pulverising the head of Aloysius Warren, a third blowing a hole in the plaster wall adjacent to the door, and the last mortally wounding Everett Trevor. Before he died, however, Trevor managed to squeeze off five shots from his handgun, killing both guards with bullets to the centre of their chests.

Smoke from the fierce battle filled the room with an odour of burnt sulfur, and Vincent Munroe, who intentionally failed to lift a finger to interfere, surveyed the carnage with his evil eyes widened. It was only then that he reached beneath his waistcoat and produced his revolver.

"Stay face down on the floor, all of you!" he squawked, and calmly walked to the vault, emptying it of cash that he heaped into the sacks on the hardwood floor. He abruptly turned and ordered the clerk and two tellers to tote all the money to the freight wagon outside. Afterward, he untied the team of horses and drove nonchalantly up the street, passing the gore and commotion at the flaming bakery. There, just a few paces from the structure, lay several mangled corpses, including Harry Hempfield. Frederick Wilson, scorched from the intense heat, and minus part of his left leg, writhed in agony on death's doorstep - in view of the two constables, who worked furiously with volunteers in a bucket brigade to extinguish the raging fire after frantically abandoning the payroll wagon parked in front of the bank.

"He's only a few short breaths away from hell," Munroe gloated aloud, referring to the accomplice he had assigned as a back-up to Hempfield as well as a watchdog. While the wagon rolled slowly along toward a predetermined destination, the homicidal schemer broke out into a peal of villainous laughter, nearly losing his grip on the reins.

At the bakery, a horrified bystander, who once had undergone first-aid training in the military, noticed Wilson's movements on the cobblestone walkway and dashed to his side to stop the bleeding where the leg was severed just above the knee by shrapnel and shards of glass. The good Samaritan used his belt to fashion a tourniquet, drawing it tight against the jagged wound. "Munroe, you bastard!" moaned a delirious Wilson as the stranger took off his jacket and made a pillow to prop under the victim's severely-burned head.

More police and medical personnel soon arrived on the scene, and the injured were transported to hospital as a major investigation of the events in Bromley took shape. The newspapers that evening and the next day screamed with headlines and articles about a daring raid and diversionary tactic, leaving in their wake the mysterious disappearance of the money and the culprit who survived the onslaught. Wilson was described as a nameless innocent customer at the bakery who apparently chose the wrong time and place to buy a loaf of bread. He had lapsed into a coma prior to reaching hospital, and the bystander who went to his aid was hailed as a hero for preventing one helpless British subject from being counted among those who perished.

Scotland Yard, however, was not altogether convinced the unconscious hospital patient was an innocent customer of the bakery. One inspector in particular planned to question him rigorously if he recovered from his comatose condition.

Chapter 3
ANGUISH AND ANXIETY

Weeks later, Frederick Wilson was aroused from his deep slumber when a rough nurse turned him on his side to change the bandage on the stump of the remaining portion of his left limb. She gave a start when he opened his eyes and muttered, "Where am I?"

"You're in Saint Bart's," she answered gruffly. "Now stay still - this is going to be painful, and the more you move, the worse it will be."

Wilson grimaced as the nurse unwrapped the final length of cotton and gauze from the tender flesh. "What happened to me, and why is my whole body covered so? It hurts terribly, especially my face, my ears, and my hands. Where is the rest of my leg?"

"You were in an explosion and fire. You were badly injured," the nurse replied. "Stay still and it will not hurt as much."

"I can't remember what happened this morning, only that I walked into the Keystone Bakery with - um, never mind who was with me," added Wilson circumspectly.

"Not this morning. It was almost a month ago," the nurse informed him. "You have been unconscious since then."

"Oh, lord, what will become of me? How will I walk again? Will there be scars?"

"Talk to the doctor. I'll fetch him," the nurse concluded, and darted out of the ward, leaving her task undone so the physician in charge of the patient could examine the wound, because the tissue showed positive signs of proper healing.

"You are fortunate, indeed," the doctor beamed, "definitely on the mend. We were concerned about infection, which surely would have done you in, but that danger has passed. What is your name? Do you recall what happened? The newspapers reported that you were buying a loaf of bread when the bomb exploded."

"My name is Andrew Grimes. And, yes, that's it - I was buying a loaf of bread," Wilson pretended.

"Scotland Yard wants to interrogate you about the circumstances," the doctor apprised his patient, "but I won't allow it for at least another day. Try to rest, despite your discomfort, and you will be home before you know it. Do you have a family, Mr Grimes? Relatives? How do you support yourself?"

"I am alone, no kith nor kin. I am a house painter. How will I climb a ladder again with only one leg, doctor?" Wilson begged to know.

"Once you've healed sufficiently, we can fit you with a wooden leg, Mr Grimes. You'll be good as new. I must warn you, though, that the burns will leave you disfigured. We can't do anything about that. You must learn to live with it. At first, the sight of your face in a mirror will shock you, but you will come to overlook the deformities, I am certain."

"This conversation is rather disturbing to me, doctor. I would like to be left by myself with my thoughts," Wilson requested meekly, secretly dwelling on the prospect of revenge against that cutthroat Munroe and worrying that Scotland Yard would somehow uncover the truth.

In the morning, having spent a fitful night, Wilson developed a voracious appetite for a solid meal and ate sausages, soft-boiled eggs, and toast with the assistance of another nurse, who told him a police inspector was waiting in the lounge to speak with him after breakfast. "But I know nothing, other than what I told the doctor yesterday," he complained. "Why do they want to bother me?"

"I'm sure it is just routine," the nurse assured him as she carried his tray away from the bed.

"Good day, Mr Grimes, how are you feeling?" enquired Inspector Leopold Koeberlein in a business-like voice that Wilson recognised instantly. It was the unmistakable high-pitched voice of the official who arrested him years earlier for the heist at Beckman & Company when Wilson had been newly inducted into Munroe's Wigmore Street Gang.

"I'm feeling miserable - would you expect otherwise?" Wilson responded, trying to disguise his own voice.

"I'm sorry to hear you say so. I'll be as brief as possible," Koeberlein contended. "Tell me what you remember of the morning this ghastly tragedy at the bakery occurred."

"I went in to buy a loaf of bread, and after that my memory remains a blank until I woke up in this room a day ago," Wilson alleged.

"Did you go to the bakery with anyone?" the inspector quizzed.

"Yes, with a man I was working alongside," Wilson answered reluctantly, regretting he had mentioned a companion to the nurse the day before. He anticipated the next question. "His first name was Harry, but I never knew his last."

"Harry Hempfield, no doubt," Koeberlein interjected. "He was killed when the bomb detonated, and it was no loss to the world. He was a member of the Wigmore Street Gang and probably the one who triggered the incendiary device. Did you know he was a hardened criminal, Mr Grimes?"

"No, he was just another house painter to me," Wilson allowed.

"What were you two doing in Bromley?" Koeberlein persisted.

"Painting a house, of course," Wilson shot back.

"At what address?" came the inspector's rapid retort.

"I don't remember the address - but I knew how to find the place," Wilson insisted. "And I don't remember the last name of the couple who lived there, only their first names, Angus and Mildred."

"We identified Hempfield from the information he carried in his wallet," said Koeberlein to change the subject. "You, on the other hand, had nothing to indicate who you were. Could you be another member of the Wigmore Street Gang?"

"Me? I don't know what you're talking about," Wilson, acting surprised, related emphatically.

"We have accounted for all the gang members but two, the leader himself and Frederick Wilson," Koeberlein revealed. "The rest of them are dead inside the bank - Sean O'Grady, Aloysius Warren, whose identity was established by the tattoos on his forearms, since his features were obliterated by the buckshot, and Everett Trevor, the scoundrel who murdered the two guards. Could you be Frederick Wilson, Mr Grimes?"

"You are barking up the wrong tree, inspector. Frederick Wilson is more than likely in hiding with the gang leader," Wilson argued.

"We shall see about that when the bandages come off your face," Koeberlein growled. "I shall be here on that occasion, and I shall know whether you are Mr Grimes or Mr Wilson."

Chapter 4
A MERCIFUL JUDGE

The days and nights passed restlessly for Wilson, whose animosity toward Munroe grew with amplification until Wilson was filled with abject hatred and an obsession to seek retribution. The pain throughout his body finally subsided, but the motive for vengeance did not. Additionally, he feared discovery by Inspector

Koeberlein and dreaded the future, for there would come a time when the doctor would remove the cotton and gauze mask that protected Wilson from exposure once again to the justice system. And in this instance, the penalty could mean hanging.

In time, a peg was attached with leather straps to his injured leg and he learned to walk, clumsily in the beginning, with the prosthesis. His rehabilitation complete, the moment came for the removal of bandages from the burns on his torso. A few dreaded days later, the doctor decided to have a look under the bandage on Wilson's head. Inspector Koeberlein was summoned to witness the unveiling, and he hovered over the patient with disdain when telling him that squads of police had canvassed every street and alley in Bromley but found no house with fresh paint. Nor could they locate a married couple with first names Angus and Mildred. "I'm afraid your story is falling apart, Frederick Wilson," proclaimed the official detective.

The doctor interrupted, giving instruction to his patient to sit up on the edge of the bed and relax for the procedure. "This won't be painful in the least, but it will take some time," he remarked. Ultimately, the physician reached the last layer of wrapping and uncovered the red, wrinkled skin.

"Well, well, well, it is you for certain, Fred, despite the distortions in your mug," Koeberlein chortled. "I am taking you into custody for conspiracy to commit murder and robbery." Then, turning to the doctor: "Discharge this malefactor from the hospital this morning so he can accompany me to headquarters."

"As you wish, because there is no longer the medical necessity to keep him here," the doctor acquiesced.

"I did nothing, nothing at all, in the bakery or in the bank," Wilson protested. "You can't accuse me of crimes that I didn't commit."

"We'll let a jury decide that," Koeberlein intoned. "Regardless, you are going to the lockup until then." With that, he clasped handcuffs on the defendant and escorted him out of the great medical institution.

Once Wilson was secured behind bars, Koeberlein and his fellow inspectors resumed their exhaustive efforts to find Vincent

Munroe among the four and-a-half million inhabitants of London and its suburbs. His home in Birmingham was darkened from abandonment, and the usual haunts he was known to frequent were absent any sign of him.

"He'll surface one day when things cool down, and when he does, we'll nab him," Koeberlein promised his associates at an informal conference in the Boar's Head Pub after long hours of fruitless work. "For the time being, we have other lowlifes on whose exploits we can devote our concentration. Don't worry, Munroe is a marked man and he will be within our grasp in due course."

Unbeknown to Scotland Yard, Munroe, the erstwhile kingpin of the Wigmore Street Gang, was aboard a passenger train on the other side of the Atlantic Ocean, in route from the teeming metropolis of New York to gritty, smoke-choked Pittsburg, Pennsylvania. There he would establish a criminal empire in the coal fields and steel mills, the likes of which the London police force never had experienced.

Wilson, meanwhile, sulked and languished in jail awaiting trial, although he managed to persuade his attorney to fight the charge rather than have his client plead guilty and throw himself on the mercy of the court. A month of careful preparation for the trial transpired, and when the opening statements were made by the prosecution and defence, Wilson was convinced he would be acquitted for lack of any evidence that he participated in the plot.

However, he took the witness stand in his own behalf, against the advice of counsel, and he withered under cross-examination when the prosecutor grilled him about his history of links to the gang, a connection that resulted in a prior conviction for the burglary at Beckman & Company. Also, the opposing barrister made a fool of Wilson with his alibi about painting a house in Bromley on the day the Farmers & Merchants Bank was attacked.

"What color did you paint the house?" Wilson was asked.

"White," said he confidently.

"Were you such a neat worker that not a trace of white paint was on your clothing, and not a splash on your boots?" the unrelenting lawyer queried.

"I can't explain that right now," Wilson stated, his words

laboured as beads of perspiration appeared on his forehead.

"And what of this mythical Angus and Mildred - did they pay you?"

"Y-Yes, g-generously," Wilson stammered.

"But there was no money in your pockets when you were admitted to the hospital. So how did you expect to buy a loaf of bread at the bakery with no funds?" the prosecutor went on. "Come, come now, Mr Wilson, admit to the role you played in the events and maybe the jury will recommend leniency to save you from the gallows."

"I can honestly tell the jury I played no role," the defendant cried out, shaking.

Jurors deliberated less than an hour and rendered the inevitable verdict of guilty, yet the judge tempered justice with mercy at the sentencing:

"Mr Wilson, you have suffered a tremendous hardship with your injuries, and the prosecution did not introduce sufficient testimony that would satisfy me you committed an overt act or took a substantial step toward the ends of this conspiracy. Therefore, I shall spare your life and order you imprisoned at Princetown Penitentiary for a period not to exceed fifteen years. Constables, take the prisoner away forthwith."

Wilson, his scarred head drooping, hobbled out of the courtroom with two officers clutching each of his arms. He was gratified that the jurist had not sentenced him to execution, but apprehensive about what life would hold in store at a penal facility with such a dastardly reputation.

The enormous iron doors of Princetown closed behind him the following day, the shackles that bound his hands and feet were unlocked, and Wilson was led to the tiny, dark cell he would consider his home until the year 1890, when he would reach the age of fifty-nine. He gawked at the awesome confines - three white-washed concrete walls, thick metal bars, a water bucket with a dipper, a cot with one blanket, and a small window with more bars, an opening not wide enough for a man to pass through. Wilson wondered if he possessed the stamina to undergo the punishment of these conditions for even a brief time, let alone for another five thousand, four hundred, seventy-five days and nights of maddening solitude. His brain raced with images of suicide, escape, old age, his past, and revenge.

On the third morning after his arrival at Princetown, Wilson was awakened at sunrise by the song of a bird perched on the ledge of the window. The olive-coloured little creature, a canary, chirped and pranced on the ledge for nearly a minute before flying off to join its flock. Wilson, amused, took a scrap of bread left over from his supper the previous night and broke it into morsels, laying them in a row on the ledge. Soon, the bird returned, pecked at a piece of the bread, and fluttered away again. It came back for more, this time joined by two others. They carried off their morsels in their yellow beaks and repeated the pattern until all the bread was gone.

Wilson's gesture became a ritual. Each night when he ate, he would save a scrap of bread and place chunks of it on the window ledge for the canaries to feast on in the early morning. Each time the birds appeared, he would position himself closer to them, whistling to mimic their tunes, and ultimately found that he could stand at the base of the window without disturbing their meal.

Then, one morning, after several months of practicing his ritual, the germ of an idea dawned: This relationship he developed with the canaries was the very method by which he could exact his revenge against the wicked Vincent Munroe.

As Wilson pondered, he was oblivious to the situation of his arch-enemy, who frolicked in freedom while recruiting bookmakers, runners, and thugs for the fledgling gambling enterprise he would some day build into a city-wide network of vice in Pittsburg.

Part 2
A FEMME FATALE AND THE AMERICAN ICON

Chapter 1
SHERLOCK HOLMES CONFRONTS A PRICKLY CASE

A severe ice storm and temperatures below zero ushered in the New Year of 1895, but Sherlock Holmes seemed unconcerned about blustery weather as he flipped through the pages of Scientist's Quarterly magazine in his stocking feet near the glowing-hot fire at our flat on Baker Street. "My dear Watson," he mused, "you have outdone yourself with this article about me solving the puzzle of the Conk-Singleton forgery. Your knack for exaggerating my deductive talents has been lifted to a new high with the statement that I was able to predict the outcome before learning all the pertinent facts."

"But you did tell me who perpetrated the fraud well in advance of many details emerging from your investigation," I disagreed.

"Yes, I suppose you have me there," Holmes confessed. "Perhaps your embellishments were justified to some degree. Be that as it may, I doubt you will find my powers so impressive for the matter in which I have just been engaged - the problem of Madame Monique Montpensier, who has been charged with the murder of her step-daughter, Mademoiselle Carere."

Curious, I asked under what circumstances the accusation had been leveled.

"Ordinarily," said Holmes, "the inept gendarmes fail to act even when the evidence is conclusive, but in this instance they have arrested a suspect without a corpus delicti. Absent a body, the case against Madame Montpensier is entirely circumstantial. So, I shall be off to Paris tomorrow, either to save a woman from the guillotine, or, possibly, to prove her guilt. The impassioned letter I received from her husband was more than enough to pique my interest. As he wrote at the end of it: 'If you prove my poor wife's innocence, Mr Holmes, it will give me reason to cling to the hope that my darling Carere is still alive.' "

While he packed his carry-all with winter garments, Holmes chatted merrily with me in his bedroom about his last encounter with the French police in the case of the Ferrers documents. "They were so consumed with the interview of the uncooperative butler," he recalled, "that they overlooked the principal element unlocking the entire mystery - the contract between the feuding parties, which had been secured inside the dictionary on the pages that defined the words company and compensation. These gendarmes might make fine military officers, but as investigators they lack imagination and assiduousness."

Ready for his travels, Holmes suggested we partake of a buffet-style German cuisine at the Sauerbraten House, a restaurant we had never tried but once talked about when we passed it in a hansom while traversing Little Ryder Street. "The review in the Times recommended the buffet, calling what it offered genuine Deutsche," he mentioned.

We enjoyed the authentic meal immensely, and on the way back to our lodgings, we stopped at our tobacconist's so Holmes could replenish his supply of shag for the trip to Paris. The shop was open late, for this was a Friday evening, and I bought six grams of my favourite Arcadian mixture, a pipe-full of which I smoked in the cab during the remainder of our ride.

The next morning, Holmes left the apartment early to catch the seven-forty train at Victoria Station on the new private railway connecting London to France's capital. I was scheduled to assist in several surgeries at Saint Bart's, so I left home at the same time Holmes did. As we bade each other farewell and went our separate ways, we were completely unaware that Holmes's probe of the Madame Montpensier predicament would involve a plague-spot in the East End of London - and a grisly occurrence on Goodge Street that had yet to take place.

Upon his arrival in Paris, Holmes checked into the Hotel Britannique and then braced himself to trudge in a snowstorm along the Rue de Rivoli to the fashionable apartment of Baron Benoit Montpensier, the nobleman who had written the eloquent letter about his wife's arrest and the disappearance of his twenty-six-year-old daughter, Mademoiselle Carere. Holmes, who had not announced his visit beforehand to the baron, found the bereaved man despondent and virtually unresponsive that evening, having eaten hardly a bite of his supper from the looks of the plate on the dining room table. Holmes arranged to return the following day, a Sunday, after the baron came home from church. A devout Catholic, he always stayed late after eleven o'clock Mass to pray in a pew reserved for him and his family.

When he did finally sit down in conversation with Baron Montpensier, Holmes, who spoke French fluently, learned that Madam Montpensier had become antagonistic toward Mademoiselle Carere because of the many suitors who called on her from rough-and-tumble sections of the city. "When will you bring home a decent chap and settle down to raise children instead of carousing at all hours of the night?" the step-mother would grouse repeatedly.

Mademoiselle Carere would respond with foul language and tell the woman to mind her own business. This contest of wills reached a crescendo one afternoon when a suitor, Jean Fontaine, threatened to trounce Madame Montpensier for insulting him in Mademoiselle Carere's presence.

"Threaten me and I'll run you both through with one of the cook's sharpest knives!" Madame Montpensier erupted.

It was Fontaine who notified the authorities that Mademoiselle Carere was missing after he failed in three attempts to contact her at home. On the last visit to the apartment, Baron Montpensier told Fontaine that the whereabouts of the daughter were unknown.

Later that day, the police knocked at the door to initiate an inquiry. They examined Mademoiselle Carere's bedroom, and, in a shocking development, discovered a large blood stain on the bottom sheet of her bed, which resulted in the gendarmes taking Madame Montpensier into custody.

"The evidence against her is flimsy at best," Holmes remarked to the baron, "and I am hesitant to accept the theory that dreadful harm has come to your daughter. Tell me, sir, was anything else missing besides she, a favourite keepsake for example, or a pet animal perhaps?"

"Odd that you should bring up the subject," the baron answered, stroking his grey beard, "because my wife's precious pussy-cat, Angel, vanished at the same time. Carere and I despised the fat beast, forever clawing at our legs for more raw meat."

"I see - it is as I thought," Holmes declared, not explaining his deduction. "I assume the police confiscated the bed sheet, did they not?"

"No, they took a photograph of it as evidence of Carere's murder, but they left the sheet where it was," the baron disclosed. "It is still there where they found it. I couldn't bear to touch it myself for laundering after they had departed with my Monique in irons."

"I shall take the sheet with me back to London for laboratory testing," Holmes advised the baron. "I suspect the blood is not Mademoiselle Carere's."

"But whose could it be? No one else has slept in her bed," the confused father commented.

"I shall reveal that to you once I have confirmed my suspicion," said Holmes cryptically, changing the topic altogether. "Where can I locate this Jean Fontaine?"

"He lives in Pigalle in the north of the city, a neighbourhood known for its sex shops and drug dealers," Baron Montpensier informed Holmes. "Usually you can find him in the Croissant Cafe, a dive just a block up from where he resides. This much I gathered from an exchange between two policemen, which I overheard when they were here to investigate what happened to my dear Carere."

Holmes then requested that the baron lead him to the mademoiselle's bedroom, where he collected the soiled sheet and excused himself. He took the bed linen to the hotel, folded it haphazardly into his carry-all, and rode in a carriage to the Croissant Cafe. There he encountered Jean Fontaine, who was seated in a booth with three companions, all of whom eyed the detective apprehensively over their glasses of port.

"Sorry to intrude on your meeting," Holmes began earnestly in French, "but I wonder if you might be willing to help me find a missing person, Mademoiselle Carere Montpensier."

Fontaine spoke up abruptly. "That wench is dead - her step-mother went berserk and killed her, then hid the body," he claimed. "She died owing me fifty francs for the clients I brought to her. Did you come here to pay her debt?"

"You were her procurer, then?" Holmes proposed.

"Her ambassador on the street," Fontaine corrected.

"You must have known her well. Was she close to anyone, a confidant possibly?" Holmes continued, nonplussed.

"Why all the questions? She's history. Were you in love with her or something?" Fontaine prodded.

"No, I have been hired by a relative to determine what has become of her," Holmes apprised Fontaine. "Was she close to any-one, if you know?"

"No, not really. But she did have a friend in America who traded letters with her, a man who visited her in Paris and never forgot the beautiful brunette with long, straight hair halfway down her back. He was an idiot for promising to marry a prostitute. She showed me his pledge in the letter that she kept in her purse."

"Do you remember the correspondent's name by chance?" Holmes further inquired.

"Jasper," Fontaine spouted. "How would you like to go through life with a moniker like Jasper?"

"It is a peculiar one," Holmes agreed. "Do you know from where Jasper came?"

"She told me he came from New York," Fontaine recalled. "Now leave us alone. We have business to discuss."

Holmes offered no thanks and turned to leave, but before he did he flipped a single small coin onto the table, berating the repro-bate. "That is all this wayward young woman's indebtedness to you is worth," said Holmes scornfully.

Upon his return to Baker Street from Paris, Sherlock Holmes unlatched his carry-all and unraveled the bed sheet of Mademoiselle Carere Montpensier. "Here it is, Watson," he proclaimed, "the one piece of evidence that convinces me the young lady is alive and has absconded with the intention of framing her step-mother for murder. The gendarmes left the sheet there on the bed for me to impound and expose them as incompetent imbeciles. Pity poor Angel the pussycat, who had to expire for a foiled stratagem."

"Should you not wait for the labouratory test to substantiate your theory before you proceed?" I cautioned.

"As certain as I am of the result, I shall go through the motions regardless after I have had some of that sumptuous roast beef you ate for lunch," Holmes cackled.

"But how did you know what I ate for lunch?" I snapped.

"Although I possess a special talent for making accurate deductions, my friend, I can hardly attribute my calculation to anything but a simple observation. See there, you carelessly dribbled some of the gravy on your shirt sleeve and cuff," he quipped.

"Hmm. So I did," I acknowledged, wetting a napkin and rubbing it across the tiny tell-tale marks.

"Accompany me, why don't you, Watson, to the chemistry lab at Saint Bart's for the verification of my supposition," Holmes suggested.

"I would be happy to," I said to accept his invitation with pleasure, for I never wanted to miss out on his ardent reactions when one of his theories was validated.

Holmes devoured the hot roast beef sandwich I made for him, and he then made another himself, saying he was famished because he hadn't tasted a meal for two days - one of his imprudent habits, neglecting sustenance, while on the scent in a mystery.
Soon we were in a hansom on our way to the hospital, bundled in our long coats and hats against the frigid winter wind. Once there, we traversed the labyrinth of glistening hallways and entered the chemistry laboratory through the dissecting room.

Holmes took the blood-stained sheet and spread it out on a wide table, empty but for a few microscopes and Bunsen lamps. He used his jack-knife to cut out a small patch of the stain and moistened it with an eyedropper. Next, he placed the sample on a glass slide and positioned it under one of the microscopes. He took several minutes to examine the sample thoroughly, and then burst into applause. "It is so, Watson! Animal blood for sure. Have a gander for yourself," he gloated, stepping aside for me to see that the blood contained a nucleus in each cell and antigens different from those in humans. Said the vindicated detective:

"Angel the pussycat was killed on this sheet, not Mademoiselle Carere Montpensier, who likely disposed of the carcass in the incinerator at Baron Montpensier's apartment. That would account for the bone fragments I recovered when sifting through the ashes. All that remains to be accomplished now is locating a promiscuous female who wishes not to be found."

Chapter 2
TANGLED WEBS

Vincent Munroe could not have been more pleased with himself, for now, in the beginning of 1895, he was a successful racketeer who had amassed a small fortune with his lottery, which attracted thousands of bets daily from steelworkers, coal miners, businessmen, housewives, merchants, and others from all walks of life in Pittsburg. He had devised a scheme that paid the winning players six hundred-to-one odds each weekday if the right three-digit number was chosen before the closing bell on the New York Stock Exchange. Munroe's game of chance became part of the vernacular in the sooty city, prompting commoners to ask one another, "What number did you play today?" Even stodgy tycoons participated, although they were loathe to admit it. Munroe, under an alias he had adopted upon his arrival in Pittsburg, derived the winning number from a formula he concocted while posing as an investor in eateries. That formula was based on the stock quotations of certain companies, figures published in the final evening edition of The Penny Press. The gambling public boosted the circulation of the newspaper to such a degree that it could pay carriers to deliver copies of the scandal sheet to doorsteps in residential neighbourhoods in every direction. Munroe became a household word, hailed as a hero of the workingman, but his wealth and fame came with risks.

His system employed bookies who collected the wagers, runners who shuttled the money and slips of paper containing the bets to "numbers banks" in homes or stores, plus enforcers who shielded the wads of cash and bags of coins from would-be robbers and thieves within the network. If funds were stolen, the enforcers dealt violently with the culprits after Munroe ordered them annihilated. This brutal security measure deterred most attempts to deprive Munroe of his earnings.

But now there was a new threat. The commonwealth's legislature had enacted a bill outlawing gambling, and the governor, appealing to the Puritan instincts of religious zealots, prepared to sign the legislation. Munroe poured many hundreds of dollars into the governor's re-election campaign, but reporters who covered the Capitol raised a ruckus when they were tipped to Munroe's contribution by the governor's opponent. Munroe's effort to influence the incumbent failed miserably, and the bill became the law of the land.

Now operating an illegal enterprise, Munroe was forced underground, and he became the target of the Pittsburg police. Their anti-gambling fervor resulted in the expansion of the racket squad, a large detachment of vice detectives who added unlawful wagering to their heretofore sole duty, rounding up prostitutes and shuttering brothels.

Munroe faced a dilemma: Go straight and be satisfied with the fortune he had, or keep his empire intact. Without hesitation, he selected the latter option. Munroe racked his brain to find a remedy to the impending raids the racket squad would conduct on the numbers banks and, potentially, on his spacious dwelling in the ritzy Hill District of Pittsburg. He paced nervously in front of his desk in the study, rejecting one idea after another, until the outline of a spectacular bribery strategy flowed into his head. He would corrupt the chief of the racket squad so that he directed his men to concentrate only on the bookmakers, whom Munroe could easily replace if they were arrested and carted away to jail. He would post bail for incarcerated numbers writers and provide them attorneys. Next, he would pay protection money to the prosecutor and the judges for granting leniency to the lawbreakers - a bold, expensive plan that would nonetheless guarantee his safety and salvage the profits of his lucrative venture. Nothing in the justice process would remain sacred, and nothing that he foresaw could stop him from achieving his objective.

To further ensure his immunity, Munroe altered his identity, unofficially changing his surname once again, this time to Arcuri, and relocating to a more modest area of the city that Italian immigrants tended to inhabit. Once there, Munroe instructed his runners to transport the proceeds of the lottery from the numbers banks to his new address, a tactic that would perplex the authorities if they attempted to seize the daily wager slips and money from the house he vacated in the Hill District. As an additional precaution, Munroe adjusted his schedule for taking the assets from each day's haul to the five legitimate banks where he maintained accounts as the owner of several regional restaurants, which he bought through the years under another assumed name.

Cock sure of his designs, Munroe invited Lawrence Mulrooney, commander of the racket squad, to a luncheon in his honour to celebrate his fortieth birthday at one of the restaurants in Munroe's chain.

"It would be worth your while to go easy on the gamblers in town," Munroe whispered to Mulrooney over soup and sandwiches.

"What is that supposed to mean?" Mulrooney snarled as he swallowed a mouthful of hot lobster bisque.

"I mean I know someone who would pay you two hundred dollars a month to give a break to certain elements of the numbers business," Munroe explained.

"Two hundred clams a month! A fellow could retire at an early age on that kind of deal," Mulrooney, tempted to accept, answered in disbelief. "Who is this someone?"

"He wishes to be anonymous," Munroe contended deceptively. "This anonymous individual would furnish me with the cash, and I would relay it to you."

"And what would I do to earn his largesse?" Mulrooney

wanted to know.

"You would hunt no higher than the first rung of the ladder in the gambling trade," Munroe proposed.

"You're talkin' my language. Let's try out this offer for a month," came the commander's excited response.

Thus, the wheels were set in motion for a pattern of contamination that would eventually extend its tentacles from police headquarters to the courthouse.

Jubilant, Vincent Munroe congratulated himself for the victory over racket squad commander Lawrence Mulrooney, but the gangster's scheme did not end there. Munroe was to focus next on an aggressive prosecutor and firebrand, District Attorney Robert W. Duncan.

Now the object of Munroe's undivided attention, Duncan was a popular and powerful politician who crusaded against purveyors of lewd books and magazines, preaching in dramatic oratories that vermin such as they, as well as other vice lords in the community, were eroding the city's moral fabric. But while projecting this persona as a champion of decency for ordinary citizens, he was engrossed in a clandestine, perverted lifestyle. Unmarried, handsome, debonair, and middle-aged, Duncan disdained women and instead preferred young boys for companionship and intimacy - a condition which, if made public, would demolish his career and his bright future in politics. Duncan's ambition was to occupy the governor's mansion, and from there, the White House.

Despite his discreet behavior in private, rumours persisted among political insiders about Duncan's proclivity. Munroe had once listened in on this idle speculation at his downtown restaurant, which was frequented by courthouse employees, criminal defence lawyers, police detectives, shady characters, and the press. "It's a wonder his enemies haven't laid a trap for Mr Goody Two-Shoes," Munroe thought as he rode in a cab to his home that afternoon.

The thought re-occurred to him now that gambling was illegal in Pennsylvania, exposing violators of the new law to prison sentences and hefty fines. So, the racketeer set out to destroy Duncan's passion for convicting wrongdoers in the vice organisations.

*   *   *

Meantime, in New York City, the former Mademoiselle Carere Montpensier, now Mrs Jasper Bernard, settled in to a sedentary life as a devoted spouse of the managing partner in a prosperous law firm. She attended tea parties with the wives of other lawyers in the syndicate, she volunteered on a church committee that was organised to assist the impoverished in the congregation, and she learned to cook and become a seamstress under the tutelage of the couple's housekeeper. Mrs Bernard's overjoyed husband doted over her and escourted her to the theatre on Broadway, to costly dinners on Fifth Avenue, and to outings in Central Park.

She was flattered by the attention, and showered her husband with affection. Deep down, however, Carere Bernard was bored silly with her new existence and secretly longed for the wild side she reveled in as a habitué of the infamous Palais Royal in Paris. So, one evening, when her husband stayed late at the office, she went to an address on Park Avenue that had been advertised in the classifieds. "For rent: Three bedroom flat, furnished, with amenities, $400/month," the notice read. She looked over the apartment, approved of its layout, and told the building superintendent she would take it.

"Will you live here alone?" he asked politely.

"No, there will be other ladies here with me," she replied, then gave the man a deposit from the liberal allowance her husband supplied. She hustled back home so she would be there to greet him tenderly when he dragged himself through the door after a difficult day at work.

A few evenings later, Mrs Bernard made the excuse to her husband that she must go to an important meeting of her charity committee at the church, which was within walking distance. Once out of sight from the sitting-room windows - her husband often watched her leave down the street - she turned the corner and hailed a cabbie to take her to the seedy parts of the West Side of Manhattan. Using her cunning and savvy, she approached numerous women of the night - only those as lovely as she - and offered them the opportunity to ply their trade in a brothel she was opening. For thirty percent of their fees, she would make available the comforts of a luxury apartment on Park Avenue, together with the added advantage of arranging appointments with gentlemen, rather than soliciting them in taverns and dance halls.

Mrs Bernard selected three gorgeous, sophisticated women from among a dozen prospects she interviewed and gave them the address of the flat she had rented, instructing them to meet her there at one-thirty the next afternoon. Her mission complete, she returned home and jabbered with her anxious husband about the lengthy list of items on the charity committee's agenda. The only task left undone would be handled after her rendezvous with the three women - contacting the tavern managers, bartenders, and dance hall personnel to offer a reward of ten dollars for every client they referred to her. "Just tell the gentlemen to mention who sent them to our little party house, and a messenger will deliver your tip," Mrs Bernard would advise the contacts.

"Jasper," she said with a cold expression at breakfast the next morning, her sparkling brown eyes glued to the plate she had not touched. "I have distressing news for you, my darling groom."

"Distressing news? What on earth could it be?" her new husband reacted, lowering the copy of The New York Times he was reading.

"I'm leaving," she whined.

"Leaving to go where? Tell me where you are going," he cajoled.

"To go our separate ways," she announced, her French accent charming him still.

"What in God's name do you mean?" he pleaded, his fingers beginning to shake.

"This wonderful life you have provided is not what I want, my sweetest," she went on. "I shall always love you for it, but it is driving me mad."

"Carere, get hold of yourself. You are talking out of your head," he maintained.

"I was a wild thing when we met, and inside I am a wild thing yet," she murmured. "Let me go, Jasper, before you are forced to confine me to an institution."

"But, dearest, I can't live without you!" he exclaimed.

"You will get over me in time," she said to soothe him. "Love is ephemeral."

"Not my love for you, Carere, it is eternal," he whimpered.

"It is too late to argue the matter, Jasper. I have made plans," she informed him sternly. "When you come home from your office tonight, I will be gone, out of your life. Do not try to find me, either, because I have taken measures to disguise who I am."

Jasper Bernard rose slowly from the table without uttering another plaintive word. He walked directly to their bedroom, sat in an armchair next to the nightstand, stretched his arm toward the drawer, and slid it open. He reached inside, withdrew a five-shot revolver, and placed the muzzle against his temple. Having no reluctance whatsoever, he sent a .45-calibre bullet into his brain.

Chapter 3
A KEY FIGURE IS COMPROMISED

Youngster Jimmie Toler, a Pittsburg newsboy who sold papers in the courthouse halls and in Vincent Munroe's nearby restaurant on Ross Street, sobbed in a chair outside the inner sanctum of District Attorney Robert W. Duncan. "What am I going to do?" the eleven-year-old lad cried to Duncan's confidential secretary. "My family depends on my earnings, and those criminals stole every penny I collected today - nearly forty cents, a fortune to me!"

Duncan heard the commotion and stepped out into the reception area of the office.

"What's the trouble, Jimmie, why are you so upset?" he wanted to find out.

"I've been robbed, right out in front of the courthouse," Jimmie apprised Duncan. "They knocked me down and took all my money out of my coat pocket."

"We'll catch them and put them in jail, Jimmie, then get your money back," said Duncan to assuage the youth. "Do you remember what they looked like? How many of them were there? Which way did they run?"

"Sure I remember. I'll never forget their faces, both of them," Jimmie stated forcefully. "They took off down Grant Street, toward the William Pitt."

Duncan, donning his hat and overcoat, coaxed the vulnerable newsboy to join him in a search, telling the victim the alley behind the swank William Pitt Hotel was an excellent place for the thieves to hide out. "The William Pitt is where I live," Duncan informed Jimmie. "If we can't find the robbers, you can go up with me to my suite. I'll give you a treat and you can tell me all about this frightening disaster."

Jimmie rose from the chair, took Duncan's hand, and walked along Grant Street to Sixth Avenue. They scoured the vicinity of the hotel, Jimmie carefully eyeing the lowlifes in the alley, but to no avail. "I think I have enough money in my rooms to replace what you lost," Duncan told the youngster. "Come with me and we shall see."

Duncan and Jimmie climbed the carpeted stairs to the penthouse, and Duncan unlocked his door, ushering the boy inside the comfortable sitting-room. The youngster was awestruck by the luxuriousness of the abode. He tested the softness of each chair and the sofa, rubbing his hands on the velvet upholstery, his eyes wandering from one painting on the walls to another. "Take off your coat and hat and I'll fix you something to drink," Duncan instructed, pouring a tall glass of brandy and locking the door. "This will make you feel better, but don't gulp it down. Sip it and tell me your story." After several swallows, the youth, feeling woozy, perceived that Duncan was massaging his shoulders sensuously, which prompted a reaction that startled the goon.

"Help! Police! Help!" Jimmie yelled, and instantly a bewildered Duncan heard the penetrating crash of a sledgehammer against the door latch. As the door was flung open, Commander Lawrence Mulrooney stepped through the entrance to the suite.

"What's going on here, Mr Duncan, are you molesting this young man?" he hollered, loud enough to bring other occupants of the floor to their doorways. "You have some explaining to do, and it better be good, or I'll take you into custody for indecent assault on a minor."

"It's nothing of that sort, Larry, only a quiet interview with the victim of a crime," Duncan affirmed.

"Do you always ply your underage victims with alcohol to get them to talk?" Mulrooney countered. "Run along home, Jimmie, you've had all the brandy you're going to get."

"Please, Larry, please forget this ever happened. I'll make it worth your while to keep this to yourself," Duncan begged.

"Now this is the second time in a week or so that somebody has proposed to make something crooked worth my while," Mulrooney commented, scratching his scalp through frizzy red hair. "What is your proposal, Mr Duncan?"

The people's advocate reached for his wallet and produced a twenty-dollar bill. "This is for you to wipe the slate clean and never mention this incident to another living soul," Duncan proffered.

"That is not quite the ticket," Mulrooney answered. "I'll take that ten-dollar bill to boot that I see in your wallet."

"It is all the cash I have until payday, but here, take it, it's yours if you keep my little secret," a humiliated and anxious Duncan concurred.

As the corrupt police official passed through the hotel lobby on his way back to headquarters, he encountered Munroe, who had just paid five dollars to an overjoyed Jimmie the newsboy for his commendable role in the set-up.

Munroe winked at the dapper Mulrooney, who tipped his fedora and winked back.

Several days after the episode at the William Pitt Hotel, the district attorney finished his breakfast at his usual small table in

Munroe's eatery, named The Jury Box, and looked up from his coffee cup to glimpse Mulrooney waiting at the counter to be served. Mulrooney sauntered over to Duncan's table and said he wanted to arrange to have a few moments alone sometime during the day. "Meet me at my quarters at twelve-thirty, after you've had a bite for lunch," Duncan told him, and the two parted company. The purpose of the get-together weighed heavily on the politician's mind all morning until the time came for Mulrooney to arrive at Duncan's suite.

Duncan answered the rap at the door and greeted Mulrooney with a brusque question: "Is this about your squad's arrest of the bookie Angelo Bruno? His case goes before the grand jury this afternoon."

"In a way it's about him, and in a way it isn't," Mulrooney replied coyly.

"Well, spit it out, Larry, why are you here?" Duncan insisted.

Mulrooney cleared his throat and began awkwardly:

"Well, I bring bad tidings. Word has leaked out about our confrontation here the other day. Jimmie the newsboy couldn't keep his mouth shut, and the information reached a certain individual who wants you to tell the grand jury that the evidence against Bruno is so weak that a conviction in court is impossible. That certain party, who knows your little secret, desires that the grand jury drop the case against Bruno."

"I was afraid of something like this," Duncan broke in. "Does this individual have a name? What will he demand next?"

"I'm getting to that," Mulrooney went on. "I don't know his identity. He communicates with me through a third person. He wants you to forfeit all the gambling cases my squad drums up, and he will pay you two hundred dollars on the first Monday of every month. The money will be concealed in a paper bag, which I'll plop on your desk, casual like, when nobody's around to watch. And today being the first Monday in February, I have the installment in my pocket to give to you in person."

"This is awful, Larry!" a stunned Duncan interjected. "It's a nightmare! I have devoted my adult life to eradicating this city of its criminal element. You are trying to force me to compromise my integrity. If I refuse to go along with this extortion, your certain individual who hides in the shadows will ruin me completely. Is that it? Is that the game?"

Mulrooney said not a word, merely nodding his head in agreement.

The astute politician paused to reflect on the alternatives, running his manicured fingertips through his close-cropped, curly, light brown hair. Then, with much trepidation, he bristled: "Give me the damn cash, you snake, and get out of my sight."

Chapter 4
AN ALLIANCE OF VIOLATORS TAKES SHAPE

Busy juggling three cases at one time, Sherlock Holmes devoted part of the day at our Baker Street diggings to composing a wire that he would send to John Joyce, a private detective in New York City who traded favorurs with Holmes on occasion. "I am asking my colleague in America to examine the records of the registrar of vital statistics in Manhattan to see if there is a marriage license on file for Mademoiselle Carere Montpensier and a groom with the first name of Jasper," Holmes explained while drafting the communiqué. "It is a long-shot, but a lead nonetheless that must be followed."

Holmes finished the message and rushed off to the telegraph office in the Strand, but I remained behind by the fireplace to make current my notes on his sundry escapades. It took nearly two hours for me to complete my task, yet there was no sign of my roommate returning any time soon. During the hiatus, our landlady, Mrs Hudson, climbed the stairs and stood on the threshold to warn me not to leave the apartment with Holmes for dinner at Simpson's, our custom on Wednesday evenings. "I have chicken and dumplings cooking on the stove for you two, with fresh carrots and peas from my trip to the market today. Where is he, for heaven's sake?" she clamoured.

"I haven't the slightest idea," I answered. "He went out to send a wire hours ago and I expected him back in a jiffy."

"Well, he'd better be here soon, before the clock strikes six, or his portion will be wasted on the dog next door," she complained, then left in a huff.

As I was to learn from him later, Holmes departed the telegraph office, took the Underground and then a hansom to Pinchin Lane, down near the water's edge, at Lambeth, where he called on Madame Adrienne Anastasie, a police informant who operated a bawdy house. The woman imported all the girls in her stable from Paris, and Holmes thought she might have chanced upon Mademoiselle Carere Montpensier in a trip to France.

"My, you are a tall and slender one, just right for Brigitte - she will show you a good time," Madame Anastasie said to greet Holmes at the carved oak door.

"I am here to see you, my good lady, if you don't mind sparing a few minutes," Holmes replied, charming her in his special way with the opposite sex.

"Me? I am ugly and too old for you," she laughed.

"You are nothing of the kind," Holmes argued. "But my coming here is for information, not for play."

"You are a detective, then?" she wondered.

"Not the official kind. I am a private consulting detective," Holmes informed her. "I am on a mission of mercy, to save an innocent French housewife from the guillotine. Will you lend me your assistance?"

"If I can," she stated compliantly. "I would not like to see a woman from my beloved country executed for any reason, guilty or not."

Holmes went into detail about his purpose and displayed for Madame Anastasie a photograph that he carried in his jacket pocket, a picture of Mademoiselle Carere Montpensier that her father had furnished.

"Colette! That is Colette!" the woman ejaculated.

"Tell me all that you know about this Colette," Holmes prodded, calming the excited madam by putting a hand on her shoulder and gently patting.

"She stole all my money, the other women's profits, everything, and disappeared into the night," Madame Anastasie related. "She came to me here, surprised me on my doorstep. I did not find her in Paris. She just knocked on my door, out of the blue. 'I have heard about you and your little business,' she told me. 'I can earn you many more pounds than you make with all the other ladies put together,' she claimed. So I let her in and gave her a room."

"Did she say much about herself, whether she had plans?" Holmes queried.

"Only that she was going on a long voyage and needed money for the steamship," Madame Anastasie recalled. "Please find her and take back what belongs to me. I'll pay you a reward, Mr Holmes. Talk to my girls, they'll tell you more about Colette."

The other women in the house remembered Colette vividly, one telling Holmes jealously that a well-to-do lawyer in New York intended to make Colette his bride.

When his questions were answered and it came time to leave, the women fawned over their inquisitor and coaxed him to stay, but Holmes politely shunned their obsequious solicitations, excused himself, and scampered outside.

On his way back to our flat, Holmes stopped at the telegraph office again to supplement the earlier message he had dispatched to John Joyce in New York.

*   *   *

In that gigantic cesspool and cultural Mecca, the recent widow Bernard, once more adopting the pseudonym Colette, expanded her brothel activity into two more establishments on the West Side of Manhattan, invoking the ire of a Mafia chieftain who regarded her ventures as an invasion of his territory.

"Pay her a visit and teach her the facts of life," he ordered one of his soldiers.

The next evening, a client severely beat and sliced off the left ear of a prostitute in the original brothel on Park Avenue, where Colette spent much of her time. "Worse things than this can happen to you," cautioned the client to a shocked and appalled Colette. Holding the sharp point of a bloody knife blade to her throat, he advised her that she was interfering with the family business of Don Antonio Capizzi. "You must pay homage to the Organisation - fifty percent - or get out of town," the brute revealed. "Otherwise, they could find you floating in the Hudson without your pretty head. We'll give you until tomorrow to decide which it will be."

The widow Bernard, still shaken to the core, lay awake all night considering her options. She had learned through the grapevine of a wide-open marketplace in a city to the west, and in the morning she packed her trunk, rounded up the women in her brothels, rode to Grand Central Station, tipped the porters, and boarded a westbound train. It would transport the entourage swiftly to new horizons among the steelworkers and coal miners of Pittsburg, Pennsylvania.

Having considerable cash assets plus the inheritance from her late husband's estate, Mrs Bernard faced no difficulty in renting and furnishing an expensive three-story brick home on Bedford Avenue in the Hill District, which overlooked the downtown. The owner of the dwelling, a landlord who would develop a close friendship with the widow, told her he once lived in her new residence. He said he was the operator of several restaurants, including a popular one near the courthouse called The Jury Box.

Vincent Munroe accompanied Mrs Bernard to dinner there numerous times, for he was captivated by her beauty and elegance. He visited her frequently on Bedford Avenue, chatting merrily in the parlour with the women in her employ and entertaining her with gossip about important figures in the city. She shared such talk with him, whispering the names of celebrities who had become her regular clients, including Lawrence Mulrooney, commander of the police racket squad.

Eventually, Munroe confided to her that he controlled the

numbers business in Pittsburg and that Mulrooney received protection money to look the other way. "He never pays for his good times here at my house, and his men leave me alone," Mrs Bernard confessed. "We should become partners, you and I, in a clever trick I have been conjuring."

The prospect entrigued the gambling kingpin, and he asked her to please go on.

"Well," she began eagerly, "I always wanted more than I already have, more riches than women of the royals. And I think I know of a way for both of us to surpass the wealth of the Carnegies and the Fricks."

Part 3
HISTORY CONVERGES WITH THE PRESENT

Chapter 1
A GRUESOME ACT ON GOODGE STREET

Elated at the outcome of his inquiry about a marriage license in Manhattan, Sherlock Holmes tossed the telegram from John Joyce onto my knees as we sat in armchairs facing one another by the fire. "The long-shot paid off immeasurably, Watson," Holmes croaked with glee, "because the date on the license, according to this wire, proves beyond a doubt that the mademoiselle was alive and kicking in America after she supposedly was murdered by her step-mother in France." Coupled with his testimony about animal blood on the bed sheet, Madame Montpensier's trial in Paris was assured to end in victory for the defence.

Holmes trotted off to the telegraph office once again, this time to notify Baron Montpensier of the good news about his precious Carere. However, Holmes would withhold the knowledge about what the baron's daughter had become. "There is no sense in tarnishing the image he cradles in his heart," Holmes noted on his way out the door.

Several weeks elapsed before Holmes was to be called to the witness stand, and during that time he neatly pieced together the solution to the Camberwell poisoning in addition to deflating the

Tankerville Club scandal by devising a sleight-of-hand card hoax. The details of those two cases were, in Holmes's opinion, so utterly unremarkable that he forbade me from bringing them to the attention of the public, saying they would detract from his reputation for diligence and brilliance.

Months passed after Holmes returned from his latest trip to Paris, which resulted in the acquittal of Madame Montpensier. The first signs of autumn had begun to emerge and conditions foretold of another icy winter. A cold rain pelted the pavement beneath our sitting-room windows while Holmes and I watched with amusement as the parade of soaked pedestrians scurried to a variety of destinations in the morning rush. "Nothing but an unforeseen visit from Scotland Yard would get me outside on a day like this," Holmes groaned. "And look who's coming to our door, Watson, if not Lanner the police inspector, with an urgent stride."

Mrs Hudson answered his ring of the doorbell and Holmes stepped to the top of the stairs to tell her there was no need to show Lanner up to our rooms. "He is a familiar face and needs no introduction, Mrs Hudson, so you may resume your chores without further delay," Holmes said politely. "Now come sit by the fire, inspector, and dry yourself while you enlighten Dr Watson and me as to what is so important that you ventured here in such foul conditions."

Lanner slipped out of his dripping mackintosh, hung it on the deer antlers of the mahogany cloak rack, and took up the wicker basket chair near the hearth, rubbing his pink hands together and extending them toward the heat. "It is a miserable sight on Goodge Street, more wicked than this weather, Mr Holmes," the smart-looking, young official advised, his brows raised and his forehead wrinkled. "A prominent foreigner and his wife have been murdered at the Grand Hotel. Their throats have been mutilated, ripped apart, and their eyes have been gouged out as if by a wild beast."

"Good gracious, inspector," Holmes interrupted, "please don't tell me the bodies have been removed."

"This only happened during the night sometime, and the bodies were still at the scene of the crime when I was sent to fetch you," he answered.

"Come, Watson! Quickly!" Holmes bellowed. "We must go there immediately before any clues are disturbed. You can fill us in on the particulars, inspector, in route to the hotel."

In the carriage that drove us through Regent Street and onto Tottenham Court Road, Lanner described the setting in graphic terms, gesturing with his arms to indicate the position of each corpse. The woman, in her bed clothes, was stretched out face up on the floor of the presidential suite, but the husband lay out on the lawn, having crashed through the glass door that led to the balcony, then toppling over the railing onto the wet earth five stories below. He was discovered at dawn in his nightgown by a passing cab driver, who turned the victim onto his back in a frantic attempt to find signs of life. It was then that the hackney driver gaped at the repulsive wounds and summoned a constable on patrol in the vicinity.

"You say the male victim was a prominent foreigner, inspector?" Holmes queried.

"Yes, a philanthropist from New York City," Lanner replied. "He and the missus were on a world tour to raise funds for orphans."

"A philanthropist, eh?" Holmes repeated. "As I said once before, the most repellent man in my acquaintance is a philanthropist. They usually accumulate their millions off the spines of abused labourers."

"But this one might have been different, Mr Holmes," Lanner commented. "He and his wife played hosts at a masquerade ball for the elite at the hotel two nights ago. Several thousand pounds in donations were collected at the dance. The event was featured in all the papers on the society pages, as well as an announcement a week ago with a portrait of the couple before they arrived in London."

"What became of the money? Was it recovered?" Holmes continued.

"Not a trace of it was found in the room, and it was not deposited in the hotel safe," the policeman revealed. "It appears the elderly Anthony Ward Hopkins and the lovely young Henriette Hopkins have been killed during a robbery."

"I read the announcement in the Times and made a careful study of the picture, inspector," Holmes added matter-of-factly. "I was planning to drop in on that lovely young lady to recover some money she pilfered from a French woman I know. Henriette Hopkins was not her real name. She was an imposter. Her true name was Carere Bernard, formerly Montpensier, a prostitute from Paris who disappeared months ago and turned up as the wife of a prosperous, up-and-coming attorney in New York, not the wife of your much older dead man."

"What? You must be mistaken!" a shocked Lanner blurted. "If that is the case, then who was her consort?"

"I have yet to make that determination, although I can almost be certain his name was not Anthony Ward Hopkins," Holmes postulated.

"Wait until Inspector Lestrade hears of this!" Lanner shrieked. "We are nearly there. I can imagine his beady eyes bulging!"

Chapter 2
FOLLOWING A TWISTED TRAIL

Sherlock Holmes fumed when we arrived at the Grand Hotel to examine the crime scene, for the victims had been whisked away to the dissecting room at Saint Bart's and the presidential suite had been trampled by Lestrade's men. "They left the suite in deplorable condition," Holmes griped, "not even wiping their boots as they entered to avoid what footprints were present."

"You must mean what footprint was present," Lestrade disclosed. "I refer to it in the singular, because there was only one footprint on the carpet, which my assistant Calvin Montgomery photographed. Figure that out, Mr Holmes, and you will be well on the way to solving this nasty riddle."

On his hands and knees with his convex lens, Holmes combed the floor of the suite, muttering to himself, until he came across an object under an end table near the settee. "Eureka! What have we here?" he shouted. "It is a tail feather from a rather large, grey bird."

"It must have flown in through the broken glass on the balcony door," Lestrade conjectured.

"Or, it could have been brought inside by the killer through the door leading to the hallway," Holmes suggested.

"Preposterous," said Lestrade skeptically. "What would a murderous intruder be doing with a large bird?"

"It was his weapon," Holmes contended.

"Now that is a theory for the record books, Mr Holmes," Lestrade maintained. "Have you any more strange ideas to brighten this dismal day?"

It was then that Holmes braced the inspector with the news that the female decedent was registered at the hotel under a fictitious identity, a fact that caused Lestrade's small and narrow eyes to bulge - which prompted a chuckle from Inspector Lanner.

Holmes next engaged hotel personnel in conversation about the two unfortunate guests, learning from a bellhop that the man calling himself Hopkins grew furious with his companion for promoting their charity by having their portrait delivered to the newspapers. "I didn't want to be recognised in London, and now you've plastered the city with my picture," he chastised her. This the bellhop overheard after the angered American tore off a clipping from the bulletin board in the lobby.

"The presidential suite of the Grand Hotel on Goodge Street," the article read, "will be occupied later this week by a New York City philanthropist, Anthony Ward Hopkins, and his wife, Henriette, campaigning in London during their world tour for the Orphans Relief Fund.

"The couple, both orphans in their childhoods, has devoted the next three years to raising money to build and staff orphanages in America, Europe, and Asia so that youngsters who lose their parents will not go without a safe, comfortable, and loving home.

"Donors to the Fund will be welcomed at a gala and masquerade ball, to which members of the Royal Family and Parliament have been invited. Queen Victoria has endorsed the efforts of the

Hopkinses."

Holmes, Lestrade, Lanner, and I huddled in the hotel manager's quarters to inspect some of the personal effects of the deceased that were gathered from the presidential suite. Among the belongings was a brown leather wallet, monogrammed with an M inside a circle. Lestrade opened one flap of the billfold to reveal a yellowed and worn newspaper account from the *Echo* detailing the daring robbery of the Farmers & Merchants Bank in 1875. Tucked inside that clipping was a more recent one from *The Penny Press* of Pittsburg, Pennsylvania, which described the first day of operation of The Jury Box restaurant, together with a photograph of the smiling owner, Emmett Tweedy.

"This picture of the owner bears a striking resemblance to the one of Anthony Ward Hopkins in the portrait that was published last week, if my memory of it serves me correctly," Holmes mused. "Of course, the portrait shows him as a portly gent with white hair and a white beard, but the facial characteristics are very similar."

"What could that mean other than they probably are relatives of one another?" Lestrade surmised.

"It could also mean they are the same person," Holmes proposed. "It merits further investigation. And there is significance to the letter M, as well as to the wallet's containing the old news item about the bank holdup. A souvenir, perhaps? We must review Scotland Yard's file of that ancient crime."

"Let's proceed to headquarters, but keep in mind this is a tangent you are pursuing, Mr Holmes," Lestrade proclaimed. "Our paramount objective is tracking down a killer on the loose."

"I expect my tangent to lead us in his direction, inspector," Holmes stated in rebuttal, with conviction in his voice.

At his office in the Metropolitan Police Service building, Lestrade seated us around his desk while he retrieved the file from storage in the archives section in the basement of the records room. The thick, dusty folder contained the gory particulars of that fateful day in 1875, in addition to the meticulous notes of Inspector Leopold Koeberlein concerning the fruitless search throughout London for the fugitive Vincent Munroe, leader of the Wigmore Street Gang.

"M for Munroe!" Holmes howled as we all gawked in his

direction, dumbfounded by the possibility. "Where can we find Inspector Koeberlein? He will tell us we are on the mark."

"Inspector Koeberlein is retired and living in the country-side, Oxfordshire, I believe," Lestrade responded. "But I don't know what he can contribute to this case."

"There is a train station at Eyford, in Berkshire, which is nearest Oxfordshire," said Holmes. "Watson and I shall test the recollection of the retired man hunter this afternoon."

Holmes borrowed the clipping with the restaurateur's photograph and we walked to the office of the *Times* to beg from the assistant editor the original portrait of Anthony Ward Hopkins. Then, we embarked on a train at Metropolitan Station to take us to Eyford. From there, we hired a surrey that delivered us over hills and valleys to the address in Oxfordshire that Lestrade had obtained from the pensioner secretary at Scotland Yard.

The Koeberlein residence, a modest, two-story brick structure with two chimneys, was situated among a row of identical houses separated by about thirty metres on a dirt road with the name Brixton Lane. Holmes approached the door to Number 4 Brixton Lane, rapped on it five times, and was greeted by a spry, tiny woman in her sixties who told him she was not the least interested in what we were selling.

"I am not selling anything, madam, I am here to see your husband, Leopold," Holmes told her.

"Who are you then?" she sneered.

"I am Sherlock Holmes, and this is my associate, Dr Watson," he pleasantly answered.

The little old woman paused and gulped. "The famous sleuth and his biographer? Leo will be thrilled to make your acquaintance," she beamed, "but he is not here right now. He is at the pub drinking his afternoon pint. You may wait for him here and have some tea, or you can join him, down the street and to the left."

"I believe we'll join him, my good lady. It's time for an ale," Holmes elected, and bid her goodbye.

The tavern was crowded with locals, and Holmes questioned the bartender as to which of the patrons was Mr Koeberlein. "He's the short, stubby fellow with the wire-rimmed spectacles at that corner table," came the reply.

Holmes introduced us and Leopold Koeberlein reacted with favour to meeting the renowned detective and me. "What brings you to this out-of-the-way habitat?" he inquired.

Holmes explained our purpose, and the retired inspector asked us to step outside. "The lighting in here is too poor for me to see the pictures well enough," Koeberlein remarked. "My aging eyes need sunshine for such a job." The rain had stopped and Old Sole was poking through the clouds, so we adjourned to the outdoors with our pints in hand. There were a few tables with no chairs on the broad front porch, and Holmes chose the closest tabletop to display the pictures.

Koeberlein glanced at both, grasped the newspaper clipping between his trembling fingers, and stabbed at it with his empty beer mug. "B'god, you've found that venomous serpent," he said finally, his high-pitched voice cracking. "Now this other picture with the pretty woman, you'd have to shave off that white beard and darken his hair, and then you'd see the treacherous Vincent Munroe in his earlier years. But that's him, no quarrel from me. No wonder we couldn't catch him. He had fled to the New World. I'm gratified that you brought me word of his horrific death. Let's go inside so I can buy another round and we'll toast the demise of a dangerous scourge."

Chapter 3
THE SEARCH FOR A SUSPECT

"My friend, what I must discern first," Sherlock Holmes said thoughtfully to me over his lamb chop at Simpson's, "is whether the murderer went to the hotel with the intention of killing Carere Montpensier Bernard, Vincent Munroe, or both. Not until then can

I narrow the search for a suspect. Each victim was entwined in a life of chicanery, so the list of their enemies is extensive to be sure. And all their enemies likely possess a motive."

"Your task is daunting, yet I am convinced you already have decided where to begin," I guessed.

"Quite so, Watson. I shall start in the morning at the library, researching the sport of falconry."

On the way back to our flat, we bought a copy of the evening *Standard* at the newsstand in the Strand. We stood reading on the street corner under the gaslight after seeing the headline about the homicides and the connection to the Farmers & Merchants bank robbery. Lestrade was quoted profusely, and he did not neglect to credit Holmes for his assistance to Scotland Yard, which was out of the ordinary for an inspector who customarily sought all the publicity he could generate about himself.

Exhausted, I climbed the stairs to our rooms behind Holmes, who seemed energised by the article in the paper and the challenge that lay ahead. He stretched out on the sofa with his violin, strumming a cheerful tune, while I went straight to bed. Faintly, I heard the high notes he struck, but I soon was in dreamland, never moving a muscle during the night, for I awakened in the morning in the same position. The aroma of freshly percolated coffee aroused me from slumber at dawn, and, as I staggered into a chair, still half asleep, Holmes was spreading butter and sprinkling cinnamon on the toast he made for the two of us.

"We'll witness the autopsies at eight o'clock sharp, ride to the library, then to Great Peter Street to post this sad letter I have written to Baron Montpensier expressing my condolences," Holmes forecasted. "By the time we are finished, I shall know the answer."

"The answer?" I exclaimed. "You are about to solve the case?"

"No, the case is almost solved," Holmes apprised me. "I shall know the answer to who has been following us."

"Following us? What in heaven's - " I began to say, but Holmes broke in: "Did you not notice the tall, lanky creature in the restaurant within earshot of our table and then in the shadows on the walk home last night?"

"No, I saw nothing," I responded, worried that Holmes's concern might be a symptom of paranoia.

"Once again, you see, but you do not observe, Watson," Holmes chided. "That being neither here nor there, it is almost time for us to be on our way."

I hurriedly shaved and dressed, squeezed a small glass of orange juice for each of us, consumed mine in three swallows, donned my coat and my derby, then slammed the door behind us as Holmes bounded down the steps.

At the post mortem examinations, we learned that the fatal wounds were indeed inflicted by a large bird, and possibly a second, because Dr Gordon discovered the razor-sharp tip of a talon embedded in the left eye socket of Vincent Munroe. There were defencive injuries on the hands and arms of both victims, indicating a violent struggle took place before Munroe and Mrs Bernard expired from suffocation due to the damage to their tracheas.

At the library, Holmes pored over several books about the training and handling of falcons, their dispositions toward humans, the diets of the predatory animals, and their preferred environments. I, too, perused the material and came to the conclusion, as did Holmes, that a falcon could be taught to kill a person singled out by a malefactor with whom the bird was familiar.

After Holmes deposited the letter to Baron Montpensier in the Great Peter Street post office, we were enjoying a bite for lunch at a delicatessen up the avenue a short distance away when he suddenly dropped his baked ham sandwich onto the plate and darted outside. I watched through the window as he accosted a passer-by, grabbing him by the shoulder and tossing him to the ground with a maneuver Holmes perfected while studying the martial art of Jujitsu in his spare time. I bolted to Holmes's side and listened to him accuse the tall and lanky man of hounding us night and day.

"Please, Mr Holmes, I mean you no harm!" the stranger cried out, sitting awkwardly on the walkway. "I only seek information that you alone can provide." Scrambling to his feet, the rattled subject of Holmes's deft attack identified himself as Lee Collins, an American investigative reporter for *The Penny Press* of Pittsburg, Pennsylvania.

"How do you know who I am?" Holmes demanded.

"I saw you at the Grand Hotel yesterday and inquired of a constable who you might be," acknowledged Collins, his straight black hair mussed and his clothing disheveled.

"So you learned my name, but why did that matter?" Holmes went on.

"Your reputation precedes you, sir," said Collins admiringly. "I know you will find the killer before the police, and that will attract the interest of my readers. However, I believe you could lead me to something more salient."

"Come inside the cafe while I finish my sandwich, for I have more questions," Holmes suggested, opening the glass door.

Seated back at our table, Holmes asked the newsman what could be more salient than capturing the killer.

"That is a long story, one which I will be happy to share with you," Collins continued. "I have been trailing the murdered pair ever since they left port more than three weeks ago under the false names of Anthony Ward Hopkins and Henriette Hopkins.

"The man you know as the criminal Vincent Munroe is also known in Pittsburg as a law-abiding Emmett Tweedy, an operator of restaurants, and as the gangster Egidio Arcuri, kingpin of the numbers racket in the city. I am probing his shady dealings with a police commander, as well as the chief prosecutor, and some judges. The woman in league with Munroe ran a brothel in Pittsburg and orchestrated their nefarious activities in London, but, more importantly, she kept a little black book with the initials of her clients and those of the officials Munroe was bribing. According to a source I have inside the brothel, the little black book contains the amounts of payoffs, plus the dates they were made. I would give my right arm to acquire that damning document, proof of the rampant corruption at police headquarters and at the courthouse."

"I have seen that little black book among the belongings of Munroe and Mrs Bernard," Holmes revealed. "It is in the custody of Scotland Yard. I planned to look into each of the persons in my quest for a murder suspect. Do any of those corrupt officials keep falcons?"

"Keep falcons? What kind of ridiculous question is that?"

sputtered Collins, flabbergasted.

"It is merely a curiosity of mine, pay no mind," Holmes retorted coyly. "Had the victims many enemies in Pittsburg?"

"Plenty," Collins answered.

"Here is my notebook, make me a list," Holmes instructed.

The reporter spent nearly an hour jotting down names and lavishing Holmes with the deep background on every one. "Now how can I view the little black book?" Collins asked, finally, when he had completed the chore.

"I don't believe Inspector Lestrade will show it to you without my intercession, so we can both approach him, you with your hat in your hand, after we leave here today," Holmes offered.

"If my editor permits, Mr Holmes, I'll see to it that you are rewarded," Collins promised.

"Never, never pay money for news, Mr Collins, for it taints the facts," Holmes advised emphatically.

Chapter 4
A NOTORIOUS CULPRIT

Lee Collins acquired the information for his exposé from an accommodating Lestrade, while Holmes spent considerable more time with the file of the Farmers & Merchants bank heist, concentrating on the sole surviving member of the Wigmore Street Gang, Frederick Wilson.

"My squad eliminated him as a suspect after he was questioned," Lestrade related, "because he is too feeble, and he rarely has contact with the outside world, living the life of a recluse in the slums of the East End ever since he was released from prison five years ago."

"But, according to the file, he vowed revenge against Munroe after the jury rendered its verdict," Holmes argued. "I'll concede that fifteen years of confinement in a place like Princetown Penitentiary can dampen a man's hatred for another, but, then again, it can also serve to aggrandise the emotion."

"Forget him, Mr Holmes," Lestrade debated, "he is a fossil, a decrepit eccentric who devotes his days to playing with the canaries he trains to sing, dance, and do tricks on their swinging perches."

"You are overlooking a crucial element of evidence, inspector," Holmes said abruptly, and vanished.

I, meanwhile, was riding in a cab on the way back to Baker Street from an errand Holmes assigned to me while at the delicatessen. I had taken the list of Munroe's and Mrs Bernard's enemies to the waterfront to determine if any of them arrived in London by steamship from America within the last month. I checked the list against the passenger manifests of three vessels, but the result in each instance was negative.

I was home only a few minutes when Billy, the page boy, delivered an urgent note from Holmes. "Meet me at once at the Shepherd's Bush train station - the solution is nigh," the message read. Anticipating trouble, I went up to my bedroom and retrieved my old service revolver from the dresser drawer, shoved the firearm into my jacket pocket, and rapidly descended the stairs to flag down a hansom to take me to the Underground. My journey lasted nearly an hour, and when I alighted from the train car, I encountered Holmes pacing on the platform, wringing his spindly hands while the stem of his briar-root pipe was clenched between his teeth.

"Watson, I feel it in my bones - the culprit is within my grasp, just a few blocks away in his apartment on Fenchurch Street, content with himself for having outwitted Scotland Yard," Holmes scoffed. "If Frederick Wilson can train canaries to perform amusing feats, he certainly can teach a falcon to mortally wound a target of his animosity. But that is not the clinching evidence. There is more," he claimed, without providing the details.

"What are we about to do, then?" I queried.

"We must confront Wilson with the data and extract a confession, otherwise Lestrade will not be persuaded to arrest him,"

Holmes proposed. "The suspect is not opposed to violence - did you bring your handgun?"

I patted my jacket pocket and nodded my head, and Holmes managed a smile as he turned to walk toward Wilson's residence in the filthy tenements of the East End.

We arrived at the four-story building and climbed the steps to apartment 2-C, past littered trash in the hallway and the carcass of a poisoned rat on the landing. Holmes rapped on the door several times and we heard a shuffling sound from within, but no response to the rapping. Holmes knocked again and a voice called out: "Go away!"

"It is Sherlock Holmes to see you, Mr Wilson, please open up," Holmes persisted.

"I don't care who it is. Go away or I'll shoot you through the door," Wilson threatened.

"But I have news of Vincent Munroe," Holmes shouted to entice the man.

"Vincent Munroe is dead - that is the only news I need to know. Now be gone or you will be dead, too!" the voice hollered.

Holmes motioned for us to leave and we went back out onto the street as the sun began to set. "He is a hardened criminal, a tough nut to crack," Holmes complained when we pointed ourselves in the direction of the train station. "I shall devise a strategy tonight and we'll surprise him tomorrow."

Once again in our lodgings after a delightful steak and baked potato supper at Hanson's Grille off Cavendish Square, Holmes fished a half-smoked cigar out of the coal scuttle and sat on the edge of an armchair cushion with his sharp elbows on his knees, thinking aloud while he inhaled a few puffs: "Obviously, Watson, my suspect keeps his falcon hidden away somewhere beyond his apartment, or Lestrade's men would have noticed the bird when questioning the ex-convict. Something this apparent would have forced them to put two and two together." Without further thought, Holmes advanced to the corner of the sitting-room, took the wax bust of himself from the pedestal, placed it on the seat of the armchair, and announced that it was time to press the dummy back into service. "The first time, he assisted me in the seizure of the fiendish assassin, Colonel

Sebastian Moran, and, this time, he will aid me in the undoing of another maniacal slaughterer, Frederick Wilson," Holmes foretold. "This effigy is worth its weight in gold."

Holmes said he would be departing before sunrise, but that I could sleep the morning away if I so chose. "We shall rendezvous at the Shepherd's Bush station at one o'clock in the afternoon," Holmes ordered. "By then I'll know where Wilson has sequestered the winged killer. Bring the facsimile with you, Watson."

I awoke at about five o'clock in the morning to the sound of Holmes stirring in the dinette, so I climbed out of bed and joined him for coffee. "I wouldn't miss your adventure for all the money in the world, so I'll tag along, if you don't mind," I said to greet him at the table.

"By all means, my trusted deputy," he replied. "Wrap the wax model in a blanket so we don't attract too much attention from the early commuters on the train." When I did as Holmes recommended, I remembered with dread how the bullet hole through the skull had been created by Colonel Moran's unique invention, the noiseless and powerful air-rifle.

We were in route to the East End at about five-thirty, Holmes tapping his toes on the vibrating floor of the Pullman car, twiddling his thumbs, and staring blankly at the bundle on my lap next to him. "Wilson, because of his routine in prison, is accustomed to rising at dawn," Holmes assumed, "so I expect he will lead us to the falcon soon afterward for its morning feeding."

We arrived in Wilson's neighbourhood in time to locate a suitable vantage point between two structures to view the front of his building and yet conceal ourselves sufficiently to avoid detection.

About twenty minutes after the sun had cleared the horizon, a figure with a peg leg and toting a tin lunch pail emerged onto the stoop of the dwelling. The man shuffled down the three wooden steps onto the walkway, and proceeded in the opposite direction from our surveillance position. "You remain here, Watson, there is no sense dragging that sculpture along to follow Wilson to the bird's lair," Holmes calculated. "I'll tell you all about it when I get back here."

Disappointed, I watched Holmes cautiously pursue the solitary figure into a mist and disappear. It wasn't long before I saw Holmes jogging toward my hiding place, waving his arm and gesturing behind him. Breathing heavily when he reached me, he repeated what he had heard when Wilson entered a dilapidated, abandoned horse barn about two blocks from his apartment. "'Pretty bird, pretty bird,' the malicious cripple sang," Holmes quoted. "And he whistled a strange tune."

We waited patiently for Wilson to return home, and after he had closed the outside door to his building, Holmes and I stealthily re-traced his trek to the old barn. Holmes swung open the door and we immediately were confronted by the loud flapping of wings. Holmes peeked inside and declared it safe. "The falcon is tethered to a hitching rail, Watson, so it can't fly at our throats," he assured me. "It can reach the meat and water on the ground, but it is unable to go any farther. Turn that barrel on end and set the dummy atop it." As I did, the bird made a frenzied attempt to attack the wax bust, screeching, flying to the limit of the tether, and jerking it forward again and again.

"Wilson uses that mannequin over there behind the haystack to practice with the animal on its killing technique," Holmes speculated. "The falcon has been confused by my facsimile. Behind the haystack is where we will be when I implement the rest of my plan."

Carefully avoiding the enraged predator on the way out of the barn, Holmes and I traveled back to Wilson's apartment, where Holmes directed me to stand on the landing leading to the second floor so that Wilson would have the impression Holmes was alone.

Holmes banged on the apartment door with his fist. "Open up, Wilson, or I'll bring the police! It is Sherlock Holmes," he yelled.

"I warned you not to bother me. Be gone, or else!" came the answer.

"Or else what, Wilson? You'll murder me like you did Vincent Munroe and the woman?" Holmes boomed.

"You have no proof. Get away!" Wilson growled.

"Meet me in the old barn and I'll show you proof," Holmes stated with hostility.

"You stay out of there, if you know what's good for you!" Wilson screamed.

"That is where I am going this instant," Holmes told him, and joined me on the landing, saying, "Hurry, Watson, before he sees you."

We traversed the distance to the barn at breakneck speed, Holmes in front and I, winded severely, at his heels.

The sky darkened with storm clouds as we ran inside, casting the interior in deep shadow. The falcon had quieted and was perched back on the rail, but seemed slightly agitated when we passed by it to crouch behind the haystack. The musty odour of the molding hay penetrated our nostrils, and the time was interminable before we heard Wilson alternately singing and whistling. "Pretty bird, pretty bird," he rang out, and emitted a soothing but odd sound from his puckered lips that mimicked a low, whirling wind.

The barn door creaked as he came closer, and we listened to his single footfall as the wooden peg stomped rhythmically onto the gravel entrance.

"Where are you, Holmes, you pest?" he called, and freed the falcon, whistling a shrill command. The ferocious bird leaped from the perch, its wings spread wide, and landed on the dummy with lightning quickness, digging the talons far into the neck, then pecking at the eyes with strenuous, rapid maneuvers.

"Call it off, Wilson, call it back to its perch!" Holmes demanded, stepping out from behind the haystack with his 32-calibre pistol aimed at the shocked miscreant.

Wilson, realising only then that the falcon had pounced upon a decoy, raised his arm and fired a shot from a double-barreled Derringer, the bullet retarded by its impact with the haystack. Holmes squeezed off a round from his hip that caught Wilson in the collar bone, staggering him backward and then to the floor.

"Finish me off, man, I can't go back to the penitentiary!" Wilson cried.

"I am not the bloodthirsty sidewinder here," Holmes laughed, pressing the toe of his boot onto the gun hand of Wilson. "You will live to face your punishment, it is my way."

"How did you know it was me at the hotel?" Wilson pleaded

while I dressed his wound with my kerchief to halt the bleeding.

"The killer left a single footprint, which could only mean a one-legged man," said Holmes, "and you, Wilson, fit the bill to a T."

As he spoke those words, the falcon cawed, took flight, and escaped into the air through the partially-open barn door.

Holmes sent me out to fetch a constable, which put an end to the case of the notorious canary trainer and the deadly Goodge Street affair, but for this epilogue:

In his hospital room, Frederick Wilson made a full confession to Inspector Lestrade in the presence of a stenographer. Lestrade took the stand in Wilson's trial and read the statement to the jury, an admission which explained how Wilson recognised Munroe's picture in the newspaper, how he stalked Munroe and Mrs Bernard, then carried his falcon on his forearm up the back stairs to their suite. He said he fooled them into letting him in, unleashing the beast after Munroe finally recognised him. Wilson further admitted to stealing the money in the hotel room, but swore he lost it all gambling in high-stakes card games. Despite the brutality of the murders, Wilson's lawyer passionately recommended leniency due to extenuating circumstances. "The defendant performed a public service," the barrister argued in summation, "by eliminating a menace to society alongside a female companion of ill repute with evil intentions."

The jurors ignored the barrister's remarks, yet they voted to find Wilson guilty but insane, paving the way for the judge to sentence him to a mental institution rather than a prison.

The judge ordered Wilson remanded to a mental ward "until such day that the psychiatrists deem you to be cured of your brain disease."

Wilson spent the rest of his years in Millbank Asylum, never again gaining freedom. During that time, he captured mice in the dining hall and trained them to do somersaults and other amusements for his fellow patients.

The End

THE CASE OF THE YOUNG ARTIST'S DEMISE

My fellow-lodger Sherlock Holmes had decided after breakfast to respond to his unanswered correspondence, transfixed to the mantle by the blade of his jack-knife - a quirk he retained ever since we first took up rooms together at Baker Street. The habit annoyed our landlady, Mrs Hudson, but her dismay was nothing compared to her consternation when Holmes practiced his aim at the chimney, firing his .32-calibre revolver from the settee or standing beside the acid-stained, deal-top table where he conducted scientific experiments.

"Now here is a melancholy letter from a widow in Surrey, a Mrs Treadway," said Holmes nonchalantly. "She misses her late husband, Oscar, who disappeared one afternoon from the deck of a paddle-wheel on the Thames during a fierce storm. Mrs Treadway wants me to locate the treasure in gold and jewelry Oscar assured her was buried in the wreckage of a Spanish galleon that only he knew how to find. It is no wonder, Watson, that I have procrastinated in sending the dear woman a reply. I have no idea what to say."

"You could tell her Oscar more than likely took the secret with him to his watery grave, but if he confided the location to anyone, you will soon surely discover," I suggested.

"An excellent proposal!" Holmes retorted. "So tell me, my friend, what item in the *Times* troubled you to the extent that you folded the newspaper on your knees and stared off vacantly onto the ceiling?"

Surprised that he had observed my subtle reaction, I explained that I had read in the obituary columns the name of a former patient who passed away unexpectedly at an early age. "I can't imagine what caused it," I wondered, "because she was in perfect health when I last saw her at my office in Kensington only a year ago."

"Death in the young is always tragic, and in some cases the result of unnatural means," Holmes purported. "I don't intend to imply that is so in this instance, but I am curious to learn what the coroner will find. Tell me more about your former patient."

"Minerva Grimm," I began, "was an attractive but brooding lady of thirty-one who had been raised by a housekeeper since Minerva was in her teens. Her father, an aristocrat, was kicked in the head and killed by a buggy horse, and her mother soon afterward contracted tuberculosis, suffering miserably until her death. The housekeeper and Minerva lived comfortably, for she inherited a tidy sum and supplemented her income with earnings she made selling landscape paintings, one of which hangs in the Museum of Art in Saint James's Square."

"She never married?" Holmes interjected.

"No, she never did," I answered, "but there was a time about six months ago when I thought she might. I received a wedding invitation, then abruptly two weeks later a notice that the occasion had been canceled - without explanation. I suppose she or the prospective groom suddenly got cold feet."

"Or, perhaps, a more serious turn of events," said Holmes, prophetically, to conclude the conversation on this glorious summer morning in 1895.

Over the next three days, Holmes was preoccupied with his investigations into the disappearance and murder of Cardinal Tosca, a case in which Holmes was engaged by His Holiness Pope Leo XIII, and the infamous East End affair involving the notorious canary-trainer, Wilson. It was early on the fourth day that I was startled by a news account while Holmes was preparing to leave our flat in disguise as an elderly clergyman.

"Good gracious, my good man! Listen to this!" I exclaimed, and read to him the information that the untimely demise of Minerva Grimm had been ruled a homicide by the coroner, who found traces of cyanide in her bloodstream through toxicological research.

"It doesn't surprise me in the least," Holmes commented.

"Do the police have a suspect?"

"It says here," I replied, "that they are questioning the house-keeper, Emma Uhl, and Minerva's former fiancée, Earl Kohnfelder. Inspector Lestrade promises a quick arrest."

"Quick actions are his forte, and they are usually misguided," Holmes declared. "I shall watch the developments closely and probably find it necessary to intervene."

With that, Holmes went out the door, off on a caper that would keep him away until late evening. When he returned and changed into respectable layman's garb, we shared a carafe of Chianti while waiting for a pasta dinner at our favourite restaurant, Simpson's, in the Strand.

After our delicious meal, we walked to the newsstand to acquire a copy of the *Standard* to see if there was further word of Minerva Grimm's case, but there was none, only a rehash of what had been printed in the *Times*, including the inspector's prediction. "So much for a speedy resolution to the matter," I said to Holmes sarcastically.

"It is to Lestrade's credit that he has not acted hastily," Holmes countered. "I shall visit Scotland Yard tomorrow to determine where it all stands."

That next day, Holmes took the Underground alone to police headquarters and became entangled in a queer dialogue with Inspector Lestrade, who had indeed taken the housekeeper and the one-time fiancée into custody, but the official police detective withheld the information from the press because his stratagem had failed.

"What brings you here today, Mr Holmes, your quest to teach me again what I have done wrong?" Lestrade growled.

"I am certain there are times when you do things right, Inspector, and that is when you never see me," Holmes remarked. "This time I am undecided - at least until I have had the benefit of an interview with Mr Kohnfelder and Mrs Uhl."

"They were entwined in a conspiracy to do away with Miss Grimm so they could share the money she bequeathed to Earl Kohnfelder," the inspector apprised. "Mrs Uhl laced Miss Grimm's supper with the cyanide while Kohnfelder relaxed at home with his wife and children."

"His wife and children?" Holmes ejaculated. "I thought he had been betrothed to Miss Grimm."

"He was, but he would have committed bigamy if he married her," Lestrade revealed. "His engagement to Miss Grimm was a sham. All I need now is sufficient evidence to convict him and his co-conspirator of Miss Grimm's murder."

"You say you need evidence to convict the pair, so why did you arrest them prematurely?" Holmes wanted to know.

"I was hoping one of them would confess under pressure, but they both insist they had nothing to do with Miss Grimm's death," Lestrade disclosed.

"Possibly they didn't," Holmes conjectured. "I would like to speak with each of them separately."

"Be my guest," Lestrade encouraged. "Maybe you will get farther than I."

Holmes chose to interrogate Kohnfelder first, learning from the suspect that he couldn't explain why Miss Grimm had named him in her last will and testament as the sole beneficiary of her worldly goods and possessions, including the inheritance from her parents.

"She and I parted on bitter terms after she discovered through a mutual acquaintance that I already was wed," Kohnfelder acknowledged. "It is fortunate that she did find out, though, because leading a double life grew less and less appealing as the relationship progressed. It was only a delusion that I could pull it off."

"If you are innocent, as you contend, what defence do you offer to the allegation that you coveted Miss Grimm's wealth?" Holmes probed.

"The only argument I can make is that I didn't know I was in Minerva's will until her lawyer contacted me the day before yesterday," Kohnfelder stated, stroking his thin, brown mustache and wringing his stubby hands. "It doesn't make sense that Minerva would want me to inherit her money, considering our break-up was so hostile. Can you help me, Mr Holmes? I have two young daughters and a little son who depend on me for support. My wife is seeking a divorce, an understandable consequence for me under the circumstances, but she is demanding a substantial amount in alimony. I can't afford to pay it unless I collect the proceeds of Minerva's estate, which I obviously could lose if I am convicted of her murder."

"You stand to lose more than an inheritance, Mr Kohnfelder, if the accusation is proven in court," Holmes warned. "You stand to lose your life on the gallows!"

"Oh, lord, this is more serious than I imagined," the prisoner moaned. "What would become of my children then?"

"You should have thought of them before you became involved with Miss Grimm," Holmes scolded. "But that is water over the dam. Now it is imperative to establish your innocence. I shall investigate your case, while you pray that it doesn't result in a deleterious outcome."

"Thank you, Mr Holmes," said Kohnfelder, somewhat relieved. "I have read of your successes in the past. Let's hope you can achieve another."

"Time will tell," Holmes responded. "I must begin my inquiry with a difficult question, and I cannot emphasise too strongly that I require the truth from you."

"Ask away," Kohnfelder shot back. "I shall be straightforward."

"Did you ever acquire or have possession of poison, cyanide in particular?" Holmes queried.

Kohnfelder paused, deep in thought, saying finally that he bought a vial of cyanide from an apothecary near Minerva Grimm's home in South London. "I realise this looks incriminating, but Emma Uhl requested that I fetch the deadly powder so she could kill a rat in Minerva's kitchen. That was a long time prior to our splitting up."

"I admit that is incriminating, for you as well as for Mrs Uhl," Holmes observed, "but I shall keep this revelation to myself for the present. However, if Inspector Lestrade uncovers it on his own, that might be all the evidence he needs to have both of you found guilty of a conspiracy to take the life of Miss Grimm."

"Perish the idea that I would murder her, or concoct such a plan with Mrs Uhl," Kohnfelder cried, "because we each loved

Minerva in our own way. Ever since the day I encountered her, while she was painting on Westminster Stairs, I loved her."

"And your wife? Did you love her, too?" Holmes pried.

"Yes, unfortunately, I loved them both," Kohnfelder added painfully. "What do you suppose are my chances of being acquitted?"

"Lestrade has a theory, but that is all he has for the time being. He can't go to the Justice Hall with that alone," Holmes postulated.

"Lestrade has more than a theory now," the inspector intoned as he approached the cell. "I have been listening to your revealing chat from around the corner, and I daresay it has given me the opportunity I have sought to break this case wide open. Not even a good lawyer can manipulate these facts to set you free, Mr Kohnfelder."

"You are despicable, Lestrade, unscrupulous," Holmes shouted. "This was a confidential conversation between me and a client."

"He wasn't your client when you came here, Mr Holmes," Lestrade barked. "Besides, all is fair in love and war."

"I would like to speak with the woman now, in private, of course," said Holmes to end the confrontation, finishing the interview of Kohnfelder before Holmes was actually ready.

Holmes found Emma Uhl grief-stricken. "Losing Minerva was like losing a daughter," the housekeeper tearfully told Holmes. "She and I were together most of her thirty-one years. I saw her through sickness and happy times, even the heartache of her estrangement from that wicked two-timer, Earl Kohnfelder. She was never herself after the romance was over. He deserves to hang, if only for that."

"It is apparent there is bad blood between you two - when did it erupt?" Holmes asked.

"On the day months ago that Minerva learned he was married and had offspring," Mrs Uhl remembered. "I haven't had a word with him since. He left our house in a huff, as if Minerva had caused him to become unfaithful to his family. I hollered after him not to grace our doorstep ever again."

"Did you know Miss Grimm made him the beneficiary of her will?" Holmes continued.

"That is the strangest thing," Mrs Uhl related. "Minerva never had a will until after Kohnfelder's departure. She went to see a lawyer to have one drawn up only a matter of a few weeks ago."

"What is his name?" Holmes wanted to know.

"She told me it was Mr Lombard, her mother's lawyer, but I forget his first name and his address, although she left his card on her bureau," Mrs Uhl recalled.

"I need your permission to search your house," Holmes suggested, to which the woman agreed and offered that a key was hidden in a flower pot on the front porch.

"Have the police been through your home?" Holmes further inquired.

"Not that I am aware," Mrs Uhl responded. "They came to the door and asked me to accompany them to headquarters, so I locked up and went along. No one has been inside since I left, I should think."

"Inspector Lestrade is not known for being thorough, but that borders on negligence," Holmes announced clearly. "Did he at least question you about the events surrounding Miss Grimm's expiring?"

"Yes, he did, in a gruff sort of way," she allowed.

"Tell me then, if you don't mind repeating," Holmes went on.

"Well, we had just eaten our dinner when Minerva excused herself and went to her bedroom, complaining of a headache. When I looked in on her at about nine o'clock, she wasn't breathing, lying there on the bed fully clothed, clutching her locket with the chain dangling. I ran to the neighbor, who is a nurse. She came to the house with me and listened for a heartbeat but could not detect one. She pronounced Minerva dead. We summoned a constable, who notified the coroner. That is all there is to tell, except that the inspector from Scotland Yard accused me of poisoning the dear girl. What am I to do, Mr Holmes?"

"Leave that up to me," Holmes said to reassure her. "Was there any food left over from Minerva's last meal?"

"It was a pork roast with potatoes and a green vegetable, so, yes, there was enough remaining for another supper. It is all in the ice chest."

"And what of the cyanide that Mr Kohnfelder furnished some months ago - was there any residue after you poisoned the rat in the kitchen?" Holmes prodded.

"There was some, in case there were more rodents where that one came from," she confessed, "but I kept it hidden in a cupboard. It had a skull and crossbones on the label."

"So anyone seeing the vial would know it contained a dangerous substance," Holmes surmised.

"To be sure, they would," Mrs Uhl concluded.

"Thank you, madam, I know this has been a series of traumatic experiences and I shall leave now to relieve you of the stressfulness of your situation," Holmes said sympathetically. "I shall return in a few days, perhaps with good news."

On the way out, Holmes stopped at Inspector Lestrade's desk to renew the protest over his eavesdropping and to tell the official there was another theory that he should consider.

"I don't want to hear more theories," Inspector Lestrade grumbled. "I have sent one of my men to the apothecary in South London to confirm the theory I am convinced is right."

"And if it is wrong, you might have the blood of an innocent man on your conscience," Holmes admonished.

"My conscience will be clear, unlike Kohnfelder's when they put a silk rope around his neck," Inspector Lestrade argued, fashioning an imaginary noose around his own throat and pulling it tight.

Holmes came back to Baker Street still fuming over the episode and urged me to go with him to Minerva Grimm's house. I readily agreed and, after a quick bite of lunch, we were walking to the Underground station for a train ride to Threadneedle Street.

The carriage was crowded with tourists and shoppers, so we were forced to stand, hanging on to the leather loops suspended from the ceiling. Holmes tried to speak to me in a low voice, but the noise of the traveling car and the passengers inside drowned out his words. I pointed to my ear and shook my head no to indicate that I couldn't understand him. "It's just as well," he said loudly, "I was only putting words to my thoughts." When the train came to a halt at our destination, we pushed past others who were also standing and emerged in a pleasant neighborhood with two-story, brick or stone homes and immaculate lawns, each separated by a row of elm and oak trees, the leaves and branches of which provided some measure of cooling shade in the stifling heat.

"Miss Grimm's and Emma Uhl's residence is a few blocks up the way, according to the address Mrs Uhl gave me," Holmes advised. "We can take our time getting there - it is such a hot day." Dripping with perspiration when we arrived at the location, we slipped off our jackets and draped them over our arms after Holmes fished the key out of the flower pot. "It's the second place a burglar would look if he found nothing under the doormat," Holmes jested.

Holmes led the way into the foyer, the walls of which were decorated with landscape paintings and a portrait of the deceased's parents, standing shoulder-to-shoulder on the front walk with their home in the background. Beyond the foyer was a cozy sitting-room with more landscape paintings, and off to the right the entrance to a dining area with place settings for two on the large, oak table. "Let's have a look in the kitchen," said Holmes in a serious tone, and he made a bee-line for the corner cupboard. In it, tucked in the back behind several canning jars, he found the vial with the skull and crossbones. "We should leave it here for Lestrade to confiscate if ever he gets the notion to visit the scene of the crime," Holmes proclaimed. "I want to locate Miss Grimm's bedroom before he makes a mess of it." We ascended the stairs to the second floor and entered one of three spacious rooms that contained an easel and a multitude of tiny paint cans. On the top of the bureau Holmes spotted a business card with the words "Heathcliff Lombard, Attorney-at-Law," and an address on Farrington Street in Vincent Square. "We shall call on him after we depart," Holmes foretold, and proceeded to inspect a nightstand, where Minerva Grimm's locket had been lain after Emma Uhl pried it from the victim's dainty fingers. Holmes placed the locket in his vest pocket and examined the latest entries in a diary under the oil lamp. "I'll leave this diary for Lestrade as well, for it might just persuade him to question his theory," Holmes remarked cryptically.

Next, Holmes dropped his index finger and middle finger into an empty water glass, and he carefully lifted it, tucking it gently into the pocket of his jacket. "Lestrade should be here to do this, but since he isn't, I don't want to disturb any fingerprints on the outside of the glass. There could be someone else's latent impressions on it, besides Miss Grimm's," he advised. "I shall also test the inside surface of the glass for traces of cyanide at the hospital chemistry labouratory." As we were about to exit the bedroom, Holmes glanced out the window and startled me. "Halloa! What have we here?" he blurted, grasping my arm to prevent me from moving past him. "Look! There is a ladder propped up against the house below the window, and the window is unlocked."

"What could it mean?" I implored.

"It could mean someone came through this bedroom window, perhaps at night immediately before or after Miss Grimm's death," Holmes speculated. "Someone who didn't wish to be seen at the door. On the way out, I shall see if there are footprints in the flower bed. For the moment, return to the kitchen with me, Watson, and we shall raid the ice chest," Holmes instructed. Descending the stairs, we entered the kitchen again through a hallway illuminated brightly by two broad skylights in the ceiling of the second story. "While I take samples of the pork roast and trimmings, see if you can locate a paper sack in a cupboard drawer," Holmes requested. Sure enough, there were paper sacks a-plenty, so he plopped the meat, a potato, and a section of broccoli into one I held open. "I shall take this food to the hospital to test it too for cyanide," stated Holmes, replacing the leftover portions into the ice chest. "A negative result should help clear Emma Uhl and support my own theory, not Lestrade's."

We went outside and around the corner of the house, where Holmes, on his hands and knees, found a man's boot prints etched in the soft soil of the flower bed near the base of the ladder. Using his tape measure and magnifying glass, Holmes concluded the man wore a size ten, square-toed boot with a broad metal heel on the left foot and a low regular heel with a cleat on the right. "I'm afraid this does not bode well for my client, Earl Kohnfelder," said Holmes profoundly. "He wears boots of the identical description to compensate for the deformity in his left leg, which was apparent when he paced in the cellblock while telling me his story. He neglected to mention the whole story, however. He is for certain the visitor who climbed through Miss Grimm's window, more than likely the night she died."

"Then it is probable he poisoned Minerva and made his escape down the ladder without the knowledge of Emma Uhl," I proposed.

"Not necessarily. There is another possibility," Holmes suggested, saying nothing further.

We left the neighborhood in a hansom, traveling to Vincent Square to make inquiries of Heathcliff Lombard, the barrister, about the circumstances surrounding Minerva Grimm's will, for it was unusual that a person of such a tender age and in good health would be concerned about such matters.

Distinguished in his suit of heather tweed, with spectacles that were perched on the tip of his nose, Lombard, reserved in word and manner, remembered distinctly the day the young lady approached him to arrange her estate. "She was obsessed with a premonition of something dreadful in her future," he disclosed, "and she wanted me to devote my undivided attention to drafting her bequest to a gentleman she said she loved unconditionally. Naturally, I told her I couldn't suspend my duties to my other clients, although I would give her situation priority treatment. She seemed satisfied with that and handed me an envelope that she wanted included in the text of the will. The envelope was to be opened only upon the death of her loved one, a Mr Earl Kohnfelder."

"Did that not strike you as odd, Mr Lombard?" Holmes asked.

"Very odd indeed, Mr Holmes, but I agreed to her conditions without letting on," Lombard replied. "It was all unlike the simple arrangements her mother made when she was horribly ill. I prepared her will as well and managed the trust fund for Minerva before she came of age."

"Since Earl Kohnfelder has been arrested for the murder of Miss Grimm, along with the former guardian, Emma Uhl, do you not suppose the contents of the envelope might shed some light on the case?" Holmes continued. "Shouldn't we open it now?"

"It is a definite possibility, Mr Holmes, that the envelope contains evidence bearing on their fate, but Minerva's intention was explicit. We cannot violate the instructions in her will," Lombard insisted, running his right hand through his neatly-combed, wavy white hair.

"A court order would nevertheless supersede your opinion," Holmes conjectured. "I am convinced there is an immediate need to view what the envelope contains."

"If you feel so strongly, then petition the court for an order," Lombard maintained. "Of course, I would honor it - but nothing short of a judge's decree."

We left the lawyer's office and went directly to the great hospital, Saint Bart's, so Holmes could conduct his experiments on the food and the drinking glass. I watched intently as he mixed various chemicals in beakers. Using an eye-dropper, he spread the liquid over the pork roast, potato, broccoli, and the inside of the glass. "If it turns yellow, that is a reaction to cyanide, Watson," he informed me. The food showed no such result, but the mixture in the water glass turned as yellow as the sun. "So now we know!" Holmes roared. "Miss Grimm ingested the poison with a drink of water, not from the meal prepared by Emma Uhl! This should be cause enough for Lestrade to set her free, but I shall perform the same test on the inside of Miss Grimm's locket to confirm my theory."

Holmes daubed his chemical mixture onto the tiny photograph of Minerva Grimm's mother and father inside the locket, turning it a brilliant yellow. "There is no doubt now that my theory is correct," he announced.

With that, it was off to Scotland Yard in a cab, the driver of which refused to hurry because the heat of the day was too intense for the horse to maneuver at a quick pace. When we reached Stockwell Place, the bay gelding stopped under a shade tree and lingered, prompting the driver to order us out to walk the rest of the way. "My horse is all in and I can't ask him to go another step," he explained. So we trudged along the remaining kilometer and arrived at Metropolitan Police Headquarters, drenched and exhausted, just as Lestrade was leaving for home.

"Well, you two surely are a sight to behold," he commented. "Come into my office, rest, and have a refreshment. What urgent event brought you today at this hour, something that couldn't wait until the coolness of the morning?" As he spoke, he poured us each some cold water from a pitcher in the small ice chest in the corner of his office.

Sipping the drink and still breathing heavily, Holmes related what he had discovered and urged Lestrade to release Mrs Uhl. "As for Mr Kohnfelder, we must first hear his version of what transpired in Miss Grimm's bedroom the night she died," Holmes said as he cautiously produced the water glass from her nightstand. "I suspect Mr Kohnfelder's latent fingerprints will be found on this."

"I admit the evidence points away from Emma Uhl, but if Kohnfelder's fingerprints are established to be there, then his guilt will be proven beyond a reasonable doubt," Lestrade contended emphatically.

"Not so!" Holmes countered. "You are ignoring the obvious!"

"The obvious?" Lestrade sputtered. "I can't think of anything more positive of his guilt - that he dissolved the cyanide in her drink when she wasn't looking. What other possible theory could there be?"

"My theory," Holmes argued. "That she committed suicide in his presence."

"Preposterous, Mr Holmes!" Lestrade debated. "Miss Grimm was murdered for her money, and a jury will reach the same conclusion."

"Humor me for the moment, Lestrade, and let's listen to Mr Kohnfelder's rendition of the circumstances in the bedroom," Holmes implored. "Maybe if his story is plausible, a jury would render a different decision."

"Very well," Lestrade conceded. "But I insist on being there with you, because I want to be privy to whatever defence he raises."

Holmes approached the defendant bluntly, accusing him of shielding information during their first encounter. "Why did you not tell me you were in Miss Grimm's home the night she died?" he demanded. "By doing so, you have created the impression you are her killer."

"Oh, lord, Mr Holmes, how did you learn of my secretive visit?"

"That is immaterial, Mr Kohnfelder. I deduced it from the clues you left behind," Holmes told him. "Now give us the details if you wish to save your own hide."

"Regardless if it makes things appear even worse for me?" the prisoner said, relenting.

"Things couldn't appear worse than they already do," Holmes shot back.

"Alright. Alright," Kohnfelder began. "It was quite some time after our raucous break-up that Minerva contacted me at my place of employment through a messenger. Her note said she wanted to see me in private, without Mrs Uhl's knowledge. Minerva instructed me to fetch a ladder from the carriage house and climb through her bedroom window just after sunset on that fateful Friday night.

"When I went in, she was lying on her bed, weeping. I tried to kiss her, but she shoved me away and turned her face. I asked what the meeting was all about, and she mumbled something inexplicable - something concerning her being in heaven, witnessing my agony in the flames of hell. She complained of a headache and requested that I bring her a glass of water from the pitcher on her dresser. As I handed her the glass, she took the locket from around her neck, opened it, and dumped a white powder into the water. She said it was aspirin to remedy her throbbing head. Minerva then swallowed the water in several gulps, placed the glass on the nightstand, uttered a curse toward me and my family, and almost instantaneously started to convulse. A few seconds later, she was a lifeless corpse.

"Shocked beyond description, I felt a panic set in. I tried to revive her by slapping her cheeks and rubbing her arms, but it was hopeless. I darted to the window, scurried down the ladder, and ran half the way home, crying her name and pretending it was all a bad dream. I pray you believe me, for that is the whole, sorry tale, gentlemen."

"A likely one at that, Kohnfelder," grumbled Lestrade. "A jury won't buy it."

Back in Lestrade's office, Sherlock Holmes stressed the importance of the envelope possessed by Minerva Grimm's lawyer. "It is imperative that we determine the contents before Mr Kohnfelder is hung," Holmes claimed.

"You are on your own, Mr Holmes, because whatever that envelope contains is irrelevant, as far as I'm concerned," the aloof inspector pointed out.

While en route to Baker Street on the Underground train, Holmes fidgeted in his seat and recalled that the Honourable Isadore Pfife, a judge in the Central Criminal Court, owed him a favour for a deed Holmes performed that saved the jurist some embarrassment in the press. "I shall file a petition with him tomorrow and see if he too remembers what I did for him three years ago," Holmes proposed. "Meanwhile, the next stop is King Edward Street, and around the corner from Saint Paul's is a new restaurant with a Japanese seafood cuisine - shall we try it?"

It was an offer I wholeheartedly embraced. "I am hungry enough to eat the fish raw," I replied, smiling wryly.

After the interesting dinner, we ventured toward our apartment in a slow-moving cab, drawn by a poor horse with its ribs showing, its coat wet and foamy from hard work. Arriving at our destination, Holmes paid the driver and cautioned that he take better care of the animal. "Mind your own business, mister, and I'll tend to mine," the man yelled as he rode off.

Once inside our flat, Holmes took up an armchair after gathering several sheets of foolscap and a pencil. He began drafting the petition, pausing occasionally to read his pleadings aloud. I made a few suggestions how he could strengthen the wording and he accepted my editing with gratitude. "You are masterful at turning a phrase, Watson, an asset to me in more than one way," he praised. "I shall transfer these paragraphs to a better quality paper, with ink, first thing in the morning."

Over toast and coffee at sunrise the next day, Holmes was busy transcribing the petition at the table while I perused the *Times*, which carried an article that said Emma Uhl had been released from custody after Scotland Yard withdrew the murder and conspiracy charges lodged against her. The news account also noted that a trial date had been set for Earl Kohnfelder two weeks hence. "It states here, Holmes, that Mrs Uhl, the apothecary proprietor, and Lestrade are the only prosecution witnesses scheduled to testify," I related. "You are mentioned as an expert for the defence."

"Probably because I detected traces of cyanide in the locket," Holmes speculated. "If Kohnfelder administered the poison in her glass of water from across the room, as the police allege, there is no explanation for cyanide to be found in the locket, unless Miss Grimm put it there herself."

"That fact alone should raise a reasonable doubt in a juror's mind," I calculated.

"Juries are unpredictable and sometimes overlook the apparent while concentrating on the insignificant," Holmes complained, adjusting his necktie and donning his dark blue suit jacket. "Come, Watson, I am finished with the transcription. Let's be in our seats when court convenes."

"All rise!" the bailiff bellowed. "Hear ye, hear ye all! This court will come to order, the Honourable Isadore Pfife presiding."

The black-robed judge emerged from his chambers and sat unceremoniously at the bench, reviewing the docket. He ruled with judicial wisdom on the motions presented by several barristers, and came finally to the petition filed by Sherlock Holmes.

"It is a tad irregular that you come before me without an attorney," Judge Pfife quibbled, "but I shall entertain this petition because the language is so eloquent, as if a seasoned lawyer constructed it. You wish me to issue an order that the deceased's instructions in her will must be ignored? And it is because you hypothesise that the envelope contains exculpatory evidence, which can prevent the execution of an innocent man? I am inclined to deny the petition on the grounds that the defendant has not yet been convicted. However, I shall reserve judgment until a jury renders a verdict. If your client is found guilty, I shall grant your petition forthwith. If he is found not guilty, then your argument is moot and the envelope will remain sealed. Does that satisfy you, Mr Holmes?"

"Completely, your honour, and thank you kindly," Holmes responded, standing erect before the bench and returning the judge's wink.

"He did remember," Holmes whispered to me as we left the austere courtroom.

Two weeks later, Earl Kohnfelder's trial commenced, with the graphic testimony from Lestrade mesmerising the jurors and with corroburative evidence introduced through the memories of the other two prosecution witnesses. Holmes was professional and convincing, it seemed, but the jurors rolled their eyes and tilted their heads backward when William Feeney, the attorney for Kohnfelder, gave his summation, reasoning that Minerva Grimm had plotted to frame the defendant for her murder as an act of revenge. "He shattered her dream of a joyous life together, and for that she ended her own misery while designing to destroy him," Feeney proclaimed.

"Balderdash!" exclaimed the prosecution in rebuttal. "Minerva Grimm was a young and promising artist incapable of such machination, whose existence was tragically cut short by a greedy conniver, Earl Kohnfelder."

The jury deliberated an extraordinarily brief time, returning to their box in a sombre mood and avoiding eye contact with the terrified defendant.

"Gentlemen, have you reached a decision?" the judge inquired.

The foreman stood. "We have, your honour. Guilty as charged," he announced.

Kohnfelder collapsed as the hushed courtroom broke into a cheer and applause.

The judge rapped his gavel to silence the blood-thirsty crowd, and then he pronounced sentence after Kohnfelder was lifted to his feet by two constables stationed nearby as guards:

"Mr Kohnfelder, you have been found guilty by your peers of a particularly heinous crime, the willful homicide of another human being. It is my duty to order your execution by hanging on the first Monday of the coming month, and may the Almighty have mercy on your soul."

The constables whisked Kohnfelder off in irons to await his

fate on death row, while Holmes rushed out to place his name on the docket for a morning appearance before the Honourable Isadore Pfife.

The next day, having obtained a court order to open the envelope in attorney Lombard's office, Holmes invited Inspector Lestrade to accompany him to Vincent Square for the unveiling of the contents in Miss Grimm's mysterious communiqué. Lestrade was reluctant, but he agreed in the end, if only to prove that Holmes's instincts were absurdly erroneous.

We were all seated in Lombard's inner sanctum when he produced the envelope from a filing cabinet near his desk. He broke the wax seal on the envelope and informed us that it contained two documents.

"The first is an amendment to Miss Grimm's last will and testament," he recited, "which nullifies her bequest of all world-ly possessions to Earl Kohnfelder. The amendment bequeaths the valuables, including her residence, to her life-long friend and former guardian, Emma Uhl. I don't believe Miss Grimm quite understood the law regarding estates, but that is a matter for another day. It is the second document that will interest you gentlemen more. I shall quote the pertinent sentences from it, verbatim: ' ... With a heavy heart, I make this confession. May God forgive me for it, but I took my own life, seeing no comfort in pressing on without a marriage to the man I once truly loved. He is surely to be blamed for my demise, and the gallows is not punishment enough for the pain he has inflicted upon me, his wife, and his children. A just retaliation will befall him for eternity in the devil's caldron. ...'"

"There you have it, Inspector, in your murder victim's own hand," Holmes spouted as he turned in his chair to glare at Lestrade. "Now you are obligated to set things straight and see to it that my client is exonerated before the hanging, which you so eagerly sought."

Thoroughly angered, a defiant Lestrade pinned his chin to his chest and spoke "Good day" as he stomped out the door.

The End

THE ADVENTURE OF THE FLYFISHER KILLINGS

Because my friend's reading habits were eclectic, it was no surprise that I should find Sherlock Holmes poring over the pages of a book entitled *Floating Flies and How to Dress Them* while he ate toast and drank coffee on this overcast spring morning in the year 1889.

"Thinking of taking up fishing?" I asked as I placed the fresh pot of coffee back on the burner, knowing full well his answer would be no, because Holmes once told me he detested the sport due to its requirement that an angler possess the patience of a saint.

"If I took the author's advice," said Holmes skeptically, "I would suspend the functions of my insatiable intellect and surrender my occupation to countless days on the shores of chalk streams, only to be outwitted by large brown trout."

"Then why the interest in that volume?" I wanted to know.

"This volume and another that was recently published, *Dry Fly Fishing in Theory and Practice*, by the same writer, F M Halford, who goes by the pseudonym of the Detached Badger," Holmes offered, without responding to my question.

"What have those works to do with you, then?" I persisted.

"I expect one or both of them to lead me to a killer, if my suspicion is validated," he revealed.

"A killer?" I exclaimed. "Who has been killed and under what circumstances?"

"Now, now, Watson, calm yourself, don't throw a conniption," Holmes cajoled. "It is merely a suspicion so far, based on a shred of evidence. Sir Winston Gore's death might very well have been accidental, yet the note he left behind suggests otherwise. He was fishing on the bank of the River Test in Hampshire near the town of Whitchurch when he met his untimely end two weeks ago. The special constable at the scene and the deputy coroner both concluded that Sir Winston, a retired barrister, tripped on some undergrowth, fell, and struck his head on a jagged rock protruding from a clump of weeds.

"However, his widow, in a letter I received in yesterday's post, claims her husband was murdered by a party unknown to her. She inserted the note in the correspondence and requested that I investigate the matter to ensure that justice is done."

"What does the note say?" I enquired with excitement.

"Here, read it aloud, Watson, I would like to hear the words with your lively inflections," Holmes volunteered, reaching into the pocket of his mouse-coloured dressing-gown and producing an envelope that he handed to me with a flourish across the table.

I began annunciating the dead man's message after clearing my throat and taking another gulp of coffee before it turned luke warm: "'I, Sir Winston Gore, being of sound mind,'" I quoted with expression, "'do hereby predict that someone with evil intent will attempt to do me harm in the near future because of my adherence to the dogma in the writings of F M Halford. If indeed an attack upon me is successful, I would caution the police not to overlook even the most obscure motive. Thoughts of a homicidal enemy lurking in the bushes will not deter me or other gentlemen in the prestigious Flyfishers Club from pursuing our passion on the rivers and tributaries in the south of England. Long live Mr Halford, the high priest of the dry fly!'"

"A tad fanatical, was he not, Holmes?"

"Yes, it seems so, but that does not nullify the likelihood of his premonition," my fellow-lodger commented. "What say we board a train to the village of Whitchurch, look up the special constable, Lawrence O'Toole, and impose upon him to show us the spot where Sir Winston died? There might still be clues there to shed light on the mystery."

"Agreed," I replied. "Perhaps we can make a day of it and find a cozy country inn that serves delicious fare for lunch. I'll treat."

We rode the Underground to Waterloo Station, then a Main

Line coach to Whitchurch Hants, arriving in about two hours after lengthy conversations about world affairs, including the turmoil in Brazil, as well as topics ranging from the theatrical plays of George Bernard Shaw and Oscar Wilde to the free trade policy for economic development in the Australian colony of New South Wales.

Holmes asked for directions to the police station from a porter on the platform, and we walked the short distance in a light drizzle, fortunately having brought along our slickers because of the darkening sky over our apartment at Baker Street.

We found Special Constable O'Toole at his desk, polishing his boots and jesting with the janitor about a football match the Whitchurch Ravens lost the night before, oblivious to our standing quietly before him for at least a minute.

"Begging your pardon, constable, I pray I am not interfering with your work," Holmes sputtered sarcastically, "but I wonder if I could ask an indulgence."

"And who might you be?" the official responded.

Holmes introduced us and there came a reaction neither he nor I anticipated.

"Here from London to make me look like a fool?" O'Toole barked.

"On the contrary, I am here to confirm your theory on the means and manner of death of Sir Winston Gore," Holmes retorted.

"My theory needs no confirmation from anyone other than the deputy coroner, and he already has done that," O'Toole continued. "Do you intend to stir the soup and provoke an inquest?"

"An inquest might not be necessary if I come to the same conclusion as you after I have seen the area where the victim lost his life," Holmes prodded. "Will you take us there?"

"In the rain? Are you serious?" the special constable protested. "I have more pressing matters to attend, right here under this roof."

"Your superiors in the county might not see it that way if I disclose to them the gist of the note Sir Winston left in his study before the fatal fall," Holmes argued.

"The widow apprised me of the note, but the evidence of an accidental cause is irrefutable," said O'Toole obstinately. "But to prove it to you, I'll escourt you and your friend to the scene after the rain has stopped."

"Wonderful!" Holmes exploded. "Dr Watson and I shall return after lunch at the tavern we passed on our way here from the railway station. Care to join us?"

"Thank you, no, Holmes. My wife packs a lunch so I don't spend our money at pubs," the middle-aged constable grumbled, squinting with his narrow, hazel-coloured eyes and scratching his bald scalp.

Our meal of breaded fish and chips at the Chalkwater Lounge was interrupted by a local character, a poorly dressed older chap with a tobacco-stained grey beard and a navy-blue knit hat pulled far down on his forehead. "Excuse me, gents, but I think I can take you where you want to go, rain or shine," he slurred through a wad of tobacco under his lower lip.

"And where do you suppose we want to go?" I queried.

"To the place where my friend Winnie passed on to his reward," said he, drooling and wiping his mouth with his sleeve. "My name's Tazz, as in Tasmanian devil, and you are Dr Watson, and in your company is the great detective, Sherlock Holmes."

Holmes and I shook hands with Tazz as I asked him how he came to know so much.

"I was sittin' on the bench in the police station and heard everything between you and that do-nothin' O'Toole," he disclosed. "O'Toole's a sneaky sort. He could have pointed me out, because I was the one who found Winnie's body. But O'Toole probably wanted to stick close by the two of you to find out what you learned, so he kept my part in this to himself. More than likely, he's afraid you'll come up with somethin' he missed because he's too dern lazy."

"That is precisely what I hope to do," Holmes interjected. "Tazz, have you had lunch? I'd be more than happy to buy you something to eat before we go."

"I ain't et nothin' since yesterday, so I'd be grateful to partake of a fish-n-chips," our guide admitted.

Tazz devoured the food and washed it down with an ale, thanking Holmes profusely as Holmes picked up the tab for all of us, even though I insisted on paying.

Tazz walked ahead of us toward the river, describing the position of the corpse and its surroundings over his shoulder as we followed the stream to a grassy area littered with rocks and boulders about a kilometer from the inn. "It was right here, Mr Holmes, where I saw poor Winnie, my fishin' mate, stretched out in the grass with his head kinked against that very large stone," Tazz explained, gesturing with his broad, stubby hand.

Holmes inspected the earth around the stone for signs of a scuffle, but time and the weather had obliterated any footprints that could have been made by another person.

"Odd thing about this, Winnie's fly rod and reel was over there near that other stone," Tazz remembered.

"Curious," Holmes speculated, "for it seems he might have suffered a seizure or grew dizzy where the gear lay, several paces away, and then staggered to this point, where he collapsed."

"That's what I thought, but O'Toole didn't see it that way," Tazz complained, expectorating tobacco juice.

"Was there bait on Sir Winston's line, or did you not notice?" Holmes inquired.

"I didn't look, but we can sure as shootin' find out easy enough," Tazz answered. "His tackle is still at the police station - they haven't gotten 'round to giving it to the widow."

"If the line was bare, there is the possibility Sir Winston never finished tying the water knot on his hook," Holmes surmised, "so it is imperative that we inspect the area where the rod and reel were dropped. It could produce something intriguing, a lure perhaps."

All three of us hunched over and focused our eyes on the ankle-high grass in that vicinity, stepping lightly and slowly so as not to trample on such a delicate object.

"Blimey, here it be! A Mayfly lure!" Tazz shouted, and reached to scoop it up.

"Don't touch it, Tazz!" Holmes bellowed. "I'll use these tweezers instead to put it in this vial that I carry in my jacket pocket for occasions just like this one." Holmes gingerly lifted the lure to his nostrils, gently sniffed it, examined it closely with his convex lens, humming a steady sound all the while, and plopped it finally into the glass container, which he closed with a cork stopper.

"Lord in heaven, Mr Holmes, you act as if it's poisoned or somethin'," Tazz squawked.

"Exactly what I intend to determine, Tazz," Holmes revealed. "Our work here is complete. Let us return to the inn and celebrate with a pint of frosty ale."

"That suits me fine," Tazz added, expectorating once more. "So you suppose ole Winnie was murdered, then?"

"It is conceivable," Holmes conceded, and he drifted off into deep contemplation, uttering not another word until we again reached the Chalkwater Lounge.

"Tell me, Tazz," Holmes ultimately said as we all sipped our brews, "did Sir Winston ever remark about being in danger?"

"Come to mention it," Tazz answered, "Winnie was worried that a wet fly fisherman might do him in."

"For what reason?" Holmes went on.

"Winnie was a muckity-muck in the Flyfishers Club, leadin' the charge to ban the nymph fishers from the Test, and from the Kennet and the Itchen," Tazz recalled. "There's bad blood between the dry fly fishermen and the nymphers. The dry flyers look upon the nymphers as lousy sports. Me, I'll fish with any bloke who shares his catch. Winnie was always good for that. I et plenty of fine suppers on the big trout he hauled in when I was out of luck and couldn't land a meaty one. I hunt for my food, too, but Winnie didn't, so I'd always give him a nice hunk of deer or wild boar when I bagged one. He was a true friend. I hope you nail whoever murdered him, and see to it they're hung. Winnie might have been up in years, but he didn't deserve to die before his time, although he was doin' somethin' he sorely loved."

"Who is your source for lures, Tazz?" Holmes wanted to know.

"I tie my own, just like Winnie did, and we both used the same materials - deer hair, turkey feathers, things I came across when I went huntin'," Tazz told Holmes.

Holmes and I left Tazz with a second round of ale and hired a driver with a dogcart to take us to the village of Ashe, where the wife of the late Sir Winston Gore resided with her unmarried sister. Their cottage, inhabited during the spring, summer, and fall fishing seasons, bore a pine-cone wreath with black streamers on the front door, which was made of polished birch planks. Holmes expressed his condolences for both of us when the grieving Mrs Gore answered his knock. He explained that he needed to hear her opinion on some important matters.

"Do come in and have some tea in my parlour," the lady invited. "I am excited that you have taken an interest in my case, Mr Holmes." She went into the kitchen as we seated ourselves on the sofa, and she poured two cupfuls with a quivering hand.

"Was your husband in good health, madam, or did he experience problems, such as fainting spells?" Holmes asked.

"Sir Winston was as strong as an ox and as fit as a racehorse," said the proud widow, a stout person with snow-white hair wrapped in a bun, wide brown eyes, an up-turned nose, and a wrinkled forehead that accented her milky complexion.

"Do you know the names of his trading partners for the lures he tied?" Holmes further inquired.

"Oh, all the club members swapped with each other," Mrs Gore informed Holmes, "but there was one gentleman Sir Winston was thrilled to tell me about, a scientist from Chilbolton, where the rivers Dever and Anton join the Test - he contacted my husband by letter to describe a special experimental fly he wanted my darling to try. It came by post in a fancy, itsy-bitsy box, which the dearest soul I have ever known tucked in a pocket of his vest the morning he traveled to Whitchurch to disappear from my life." The bereaved woman suddenly broke into tears and sobs, wailing, which prompted her older sister to emerge from another room and instruct Holmes to cease his interview. "She has suffered enough pain for now, so please come back on a later day," the protective sibling ordered, and we immediately obeyed her wish, returning to Baker Street.

Once at home, Holmes tinkered with his chemicals at the acid-stained, deal-top table to analyse an oily film on the Mayfly replica in the vial.

"The substance exudes a hint of an aroma I thought I recognised from my samples of rare, deadly toxins that I keep in the jars on the top shelf of the corner cupboard," he related. "If I am not mistaken, the odour reminded me of an oleander blossom, the secretion from which can be absorbed rapidly into the circulatory system."

"And it can induce erratic breathing, weakness, and an irregular heartbeat," I chimed in. "How will you establish that the Mayfly imitation contained oleander oil?"

"I devised a formula with my liquids to positively identify it by the colour the solution turns after I immerse the lure," Holmes boasted, "but I must first refer to my notes of every ingredient before I can perform a test."

He adjourned to the settee with his thick folder labeled "Poison Detectors," thumbing through several pages, reading voraciously, until he came across an entry for oleander. "Ah-ha, here it is: A little of this, a little of that, some of this, some of that, plus three cubic centimeters of vanilla extract. Watson, do we have it in your spice collection in the cabinet above the wood stove?"

"Yes, I believe so. I'll fetch it," I offered.

Holmes concocted his solution in a beaker, submerged the lure, agitated it slightly, and paused. "Now we wait for a moment, and if the liquid becomes bright orange, then the substance is definitely oleander," he declared. "There! Verified!"

"You marvel me once again, Holmes, with your ingenious methods," I remarked, clapping. "All you must do now is find a suspect who has been to the tropics, where the oleander plant thrives."

"Or perhaps a scientist who has reproduced an identical climate in England, such as in an arbouretum," he postulated.

That evening, I was perusing our copy of the *Times*, which had been neglected that morning, when an article jumped off the page. "See here, Holmes, incredible news - another fisherman has been found dead, drowned in the Itchen. No foul play is evidenced, according to the deputy coroner."

"Go on, what else does it say?" Holmes begged to learn.

I continued with my summary: "The story names the victim, Kenneth Latta, aged fifty-four, of New Alresford, in Hampshire, who was wading in the water when apparently his ailing heart gave out, causing him to fall face down in the crystal-clear water."

"Does the account mention a next of kin?" Holmes questioned.

"Yes," I responded, "his sole surviving relative is a brother, Adrian, from the hamlet of Tichborne."

"We shall visit him first tomorrow, then the deputy coroner, and maybe Special Constable O'Toole," Holmes foretold. "I shall enjoy another debate with O'Toole. But, on second thought, he is the type who is so narrow-minded that he will refuse to listen to reason."

Early in the morning, after a light breakfast, we took transportation to the southern countryside again, arriving in Tichborne at about nine-thirty and finding Adrian Latta's two-story frame house with ease. We had received word of its location from a clerk sweeping the walkway in front of a small grocery, a young chap who cautioned us not to bother Mr Latta with trifles because there had been a death in the family.

"He's lost his only brother in a tragic way, so if you're going there to collect on a debt, you'd best postpone it," the clerk commanded.

"We are not agents of a creditor. It is about his brother that we want to see him," Holmes apprised the fellow.

"Well, I guess it's alright, then," he allowed.

A despondent Adrian Latta admitted us to his home, puzzled by the appearance of a private detective and a physician at his door. "What's this all about, may I ask?" he began. "The police are satisfied that my brother's drowning was due to a heart attack."

"I am trying to discern if the heart attack was brought about by something unnatural," Holmes stated with a serious expression in his dark eyes.

"Unnatural? Like what?" Mr Latta quizzed.

"A poison possibly," Holmes implied.

"A poison? How could it be? Kenneth never dabbled with poisons. He was a night watchman for the railroad who fished for trout every waking hour," the brother maintained. "I and many of his friends buried him only yesterday, without an enemy in the world, so how could he have been poisoned?"

"Have the police gone through his house?" Holmes pried.

"No, they didn't see a need," Mr Latta acknowledged.

"Would you mind if I did?" Holmes asked.

"What do you expect to find? My brother lived simply and had no valuables," Mr Latta quarreled.

"I would look for a letter from a scientist in Chilbolton," Holmes revealed. "Was your brother a member of the Flyfishers Club?"

"He was an active member, and what has that to do with your involvement?" Mr Latta demanded. "And who is this scientist you think corresponded with Kenneth? What is his involvement?"

"I can answer your questions when I reap the benefit of more data, sir," said Holmes apologetically, "but for the time being, please bear with me. Do the police have custody of your brother's tackle?"

"I suppose so, I never thought to ask for it," Mr Latta responded. "If you want to see inside my brother's tiny house, I am going there today to inventory the contents. I am the executor of his estate. You're welcome to ride along in my wagon."

"You are very gracious," Holmes said to compliment the man and to accept his offer. "One final question: Was your brother outspoken about the use of a wet fly, a nymph?"

"Very few things made him angry, but the presence of a wet fly fisherman on a chalk stream was one thing for sure," Mr Latta disclosed. "He pushed for a law to prohibit them from using their technique on the rivers and tributaries in all of south England."

The road from Tichborne to New Alresford followed the river bed, winding its way through woodlands, dotted with isolated houses in need of repair, and through open spaces, covered with tall grass and high mounds. The horse pulling the wagon trudged along as if it knew the terrain, and finally came to a halt at the entrance to a modest bungalow with overgrown shrubs and windows without curtains.

"This is where Kenneth lived, God rest his spirit," murmured the brother as we all climbed down from the wagon and went inside through an unlocked front door. Sparsely furnished, the residence was neat and clean, save for a dirty dish and a fork in the sink.

On the kitchen table, Holmes found what he had hoped to

find, an envelope with a letter from Chilbolton, postmarked with a date that preceded Kenneth Latta's death by a single day. I craned my neck over Holmes's shoulder to read the message. Here is what it said:

"Dear Mr Latta,

"I have never made your acquaintance, so allow me to introduce myself. I am an aquatic biologist and a botanist by profession, as well as an avid angler in my pastime, like yourself. I have never fished in your area of the River Itchen and I am curious to know if a special experimental dry fly I have tied will attract the trout as far upstream as where you live.

"Please try it out at your earliest convenience. If you are successful with this Mayfly lure, which I am sending in a separate parcel, please write to me with the details - and you may keep the fly for as long as it lasts.

"Wishing you the best of luck, I am

"Alfred Nicholls III

"1223 Harrow Weald

"Chilbolton, Hampshire"

Holmes handed the correspondence to Adrian Latta and he read it with awe. "How did you know about this, Mr Holmes?" he pleaded.

"I deduced its existence based upon evidence in another suspicious death that I am investigating," said Holmes to enlighten the perplexed relative. Said he:

"Then you believe my brother's demise to be suspicious? But the officials - "

"The officials are wrong in their assessment of both situations," Holmes interrupted. "I shall intervene and insist upon an inquest in your brother's case and in the other. It would be helpful if you joined me in such a request."

"I'll gladly do it so we can get to the bottom of all this," Mr Latta concurred.

We aided him in the sad duty of listing all of the deceased's possessions in the domicile, next departing to a livery stable to rent a horse and buggy. Our conveyance would deliver us to a town downstream, Avington, in the upper Itchen Valley, where a deputy coroner, Dr Morris March, had performed the autopsy on Kenneth Latta's cadaver.

In his pristine office, brightly decorated with photographs of himself on horseback at dressage events, Dr March staunchly defended his ruling of accidental drowning, even in the face of Holmes's recital of his findings thus far.

"The lungs were saturated and there was no irregularity uncovered in the microscopic examination of the blood," he proclaimed. "No, Mr Holmes, your rendition of the conditions leading to Mr Latta's heart failure is not compelling. In fact, it is far-fetched. Your theory is flimsy."

"Oleander poisoning would not become apparent in a routine examination of the blood," I interjected.

"Oh, I'll accept that, doctor, but modern as we may be in our medical practices today, there is no test available to detect the presence of oleandrin as a cardiac glycoside."

"I take it that you are rejecting my proposal of an inquest," Holmes reacted.

"An inquest is out of the question," Dr March agreed. "I have sick patients to attend, and you are usurping their time. Good day, gentlemen."

"Inhospitable territory," Holmes griped as we rode in the carriage back to the livery stable in New Alresford. "The officials in London will at least acquiesce when I accommodate them with hard evidence. Possibly the special constable who looked into the drowning can be persuaded to probe further."

Holmes discovered an ally in Special Constable Mark Sidner, an affable and eager policeman in his early thirties who said he was honoured to meet the consulting detective featured in my magazine articles. "I knew there was something peculiar about the case from the start," he confided, "but when Dr March issued his decision that the death was not dubious, my hands were tied."

"What made you perceive the case to be peculiar?" Holmes led him on.

"Well, the victim was not wearing waders, yet he was found in the water, not on the shore where his fly rod and reel lay," the youthful officer explained, adding: "That was unusual, but the most mysterious aspect of the whole story is that his line had no bait. Instead, the lure was clutched between his thumb and forefinger, gripped so tightly I had to pry it loose. And a minute or so after I did, I grew ill - the ground around me began to swirl, I could feel my heart throbbing, and my breathing became laboured. I thought the lure might contain some sort of harmful, potent substance, so I secured it in an envelope, and here it remains in my top drawer. I am going to send it off to a labouratory to have it analysed."

"Which might not be necessary," said Holmes confidently. "You see, I am investigating a second case with similar circumstances, and I already have analysed the lure in that matter. It was coated with oleander oil, the sap from the blossom of an exotic tropical plant that can be lethal through transcutaneous absorption."

"Trans what?" Sidner blurted.

"Absorption through the skin and into the bloodstream," Holmes expounded to clarify his assertion. "As in the other case, the deceased was killed by someone who had knowledge the Mayfly is the trout's favourite insect at this time of year, someone also familiar with transcutaneous absorption."

"Golly, Mr Holmes, I shall make Dr March aware of this right away," the special constable averred.

"He already has been alerted, and he has denounced my data," Holmes growled.

"What if another physician, such as Dr Watson, tried to convince him to change his mind?" Sidner recommended.

"I have tried," I grumbled, "but the man is intransigent."

"So is the special constable in Whitchurch, where the other murder occurred," Holmes groused.

"What a dilemma!" the officer exclaimed. "Two killings and no one in authority to trust an expert!"

"We could force the issue and appeal to a judge to order an inquest," Holmes suggested. "I even know the name of the suspect."

"Who is it, Mr Holmes, please tell me," Sidner asked with emotion.

"It is a scientist from Chilbolton, Alfred Nicholls III," Holmes disclosed, unfolding the letter to Latta and placing it on

Sidner's desk.

"This is a crucial piece of evidence, a nail in the coffin!" Sidner ejaculated after reviewing the letter's content. "What was his motive, if you know?"

"It seems trivial, but I believe he wished to silence Mr Latta and Sir Winston Gore, the other victim, in their quest to ban wet fly fishermen from the rivers and tributary streams," Holmes assumed. "I shall know for certain after I confront him."

"Don't count me out of that action," Sidner insisted. "Despite the deputy coroner's opinion, I am obliged to follow the evidence wherever it might lead. I know a judge empathetic toward the police and their work. He might see our dilemma and order the inquest."

"Excellent!" Holmes cried. "We should prepare a motion and file it in his court."

"Better yet, we can float the idea past him at supper tonight. He is my father," beamed the young special constable.

Ecstatic, Holmes shook Sidner's hand vigorously and bounded from the police station after jotting down his address and arranging to meet him at his home at six o'clock. Outside, Holmes and I filled our pipes and reclined on a bench situated at the opening to a pleasant, small park, where a teen-aged girl wearing a yellow dress was exercising an overweight Saint Bernard with two energetic puppies running in circles around them. "Life goes on, as if the cruel departure of two human beings from this earth never amounted to a tinker's dam," Holmes philosophised. "I am astonished, Watson, at how insignificant our legacies can be."

"And at how unexpectedly they can come about," I said to finish the thought. "I doubt Kenneth Latta or Sir Winston Gore entertained such notions when they arose on the morning of their last day on the planet."

"Enough of this morbid palaver!" Holmes spouted. "I observed the sign on a tobacconist's shop in the village square when we rode into town. Let's see if he sells your Arcadia mixture and an imported Virginia blend I have been thinking about giving a whirl. Even if he does not have them in stock, I'll purchase a few grams of chewing tobacco that I intend to present to our friend Tazz when we gather at the inquest. I am positive there will be one."

After our journey on foot to the tobacconist, Holmes and I went directly to the address in his notebook, because the dinner hour approached. We were ushered into the foyer of Judge Matthew Sidner's spacious dwelling by a butler in a black business suit and high shirt collar, an exquisite red cravat tied to perfection around his neck. "Go right in to the dining room ahead and to the left, the honourable Judge Sidner and his son are expecting you," the butler stated in a prim manner with a cockney pronunciation in his instruction.

"Mr Holmes, Dr Watson, it is my privilege to make your acquaintance," Judge Sidner began as the formalities were spoken softly by his son. "Mark tells me you are in the process of solving crimes that Dr March and Special Constable O'Toole deny took place. Morris March is arrogant and bull-headed, and this would not be the first time he has erred. Lawrence O'Toole is haphazard and allergic to the toils of a policeman."

Holmes was taken aback by the jurist's frankness, and said as much.

"I prefer brevity and getting to the crux of a problem," Judge Sidner informed him, inviting us to be seated and to drink a glass of sherry before the meal was served. "While we imbibe, you can educate me on the particulars of your endeavours."

Holmes went to great lengths to justify overruling the conclusions of the authorities in both deaths, stressing the relevance of the letters each victim received a day prior to their expiring, as well as the gifts of Mayfly lures, the analysis he conducted on the toxic substance, and the controversy over the wet fly versus the dry fly.

"Mr Holmes, you have established sufficient probable cause to warrant taking this cunning scientist into custody, let alone enough evidence to substantiate a plea for an inquest," Judge Sidner decided after listening to Holmes's version of the facts. "Come to my chambers tomorrow with a motion on paper and a brief in support of it. I'll grant your request and issue a writ forthwith."

After we feasted on roasted venison, baked sweet potatoes, buttered cauliflower, and freshly-made raisin bread, plus apple pie alamode for dessert, Mark Sidner extended an invitation for Holmes and me to spend the night in his father's guest house, which would spare us traveling the long distance back to Baker Street, only to return to New Alresford at daybreak.

We accepted the offer with gratitude, whereupon the special constable and Holmes proceeded to compose the pleadings for Holmes's appointment in court. They put the final period on the paperwork at about midnight, but Holmes remained awake in the darkened guest house drawing room, pacing and mumbling in anticipation of conflict with the treacherous Alfred Nicholls III.

After a hearty breakfast, we rode in the judge's brougham to his chambers, where he authored a writ dictating that the county coroner "convene an inquest into these two deaths at the earliest date a jury can be assembled within your jurisdiction, and summon as a witness Mr Sherlock Holmes of 221B Baker Street, London."

"Shall we venture into Chilbolton to hear the rejoinder?" Holmes propositioned as we stepped into the street.

"I'm game!" Mark Sidner announced, inhaling.

"By all means, Holmes, it promises to be the climax of your efforts," I added.

As we rode on the train, Holmes explained his strategy for approaching the suspect, reckoning him to be a clever adversary and unlikely to confess under routine questioning. "It is the element of surprise that will render him vulnerable," Holmes predicted.

Nicholls, we learned from a uniformed constable on patrol in Chilbolton, lived in a manor house two kilometers from the train station, so we walked to the nearby livery stable and acquired a four-seat carriage with a driver to travel to 1223 Harrow Weald. As the address came within our view, Holmes pointed to a vast glasshouse behind the unfortified, Elizabethan-style, grey stone mansion. "I would wager a half-crown that we shall discover he grows tropical plants in that conservatory," Holmes prognosticated. "Before we ring the bell, I'll take a gander inside. Driver, stop here, don't go any closer just yet."

Holmes leaped from the vehicle, jogged the distance to a side door of the hothouse complex, and disappeared from our sight. Inside, he was surrounded by a veritable jungle of greenery from the southern hemisphere. Startled by Holmes's presence, an elderly man dressed in coveralls who was irrigating the leafy crops emphatically expressed a desire to know what the intrusion was all about.

"Mr Nicholls, I presume?" Holmes inferred, not the least unnerved to find the enclosure occupied.

"No, Professor Nicholls is in his study. I am Douglas, his servant," the old man advised. "Who are you?"

Holmes manufactured a false name and said that he was with two other gentlemen who had business with Nicholls. "Douglas, does the professor raise oleander?"

"Oh, yes, he has several such organisms in various stages of development," Douglas volunteered. "He has been published on the subject. Is your party from the university?"

"No, we are from the Flyfishers Club," Holmes lied. "We want the professor to join our ranks."

"But Professor Nicholls is not a fisherman. He studies fish, he does not catch them for sport," Douglas bristled.

"I see," said Holmes, acting mystified. "I'll get the other gentlemen and meet you at the front door of the professor's home. Then you can announce us"

"Very good, sir," Douglas said in approval.

Holmes returned to the carriage and relayed the dialogue with Douglas. Then, our trio was escorted by the servant into Nicholls's study, an ante-room lined by a huge aquarium containing an assortment of brilliantly coloured life forms, the likes of which none of us had ever seen. We were mesmerised by the activity in the long tank, hardly taking notice of the tiny, silver-haired figure behind the oversized oak desk.

Nicholls, who had retired from teaching ten years earlier, greeted us warmly and wondered why a delegation from the Flyfishers Club was interested in counting him as a member.

"Actually, we were also sent to decipher what you know of two founding brethren in our group, Kenneth Latta of New Alresford and Sir Winston Gore of Ashe," Holmes spoke up.

"I've never heard the names before this," Nicholls claimed, a look of puzzlement crossing his countenance.

"You posted letters to them within the month," Holmes countered, "like this one," and he held out the message to Latta at

Nicholls's eye level.

"Let me have a closer inspection of that," Nicholls snarled, snatching the sheet from Holmes's hand. The suspect fumbled with a pair of spectacles in his desk drawer and brought the letter nearer to his broad nose. "This is not my handwriting. The penmanship is too perfect!" he roared. "Someone is impersonating me! What is the meaning of this?"

"Then you did not send Mayfly lures to these two members of our club?" Holmes further probed.

"Absolutely not!" Nicholls snorted. "I am in no way a sport fisherman. And I would not know how to begin making a Mayfly lure. Who could be behind this? Do you have any inkling?"

"No, but perhaps you already know the answer without it occurring to you," Holmes went on. "Who besides Douglas has access to your arbouretum?"

"Only a few of my former students," Nicholls answered. "One of them, in fact, is a fishing enthusiast - Walter Pincus of Winchester, a horticulturist for the government. Could he be the imposter? For what reason?"

"We shall be back with an explanation in the near future, professor," Holmes pledged. "We must be off to Winchester without delay."

The three of us left the retired educator in a state of confusion. We scurried into the carriage and rode off toward the train station for an excursion into Winchester.

Two hours later, we stood on the front stoop at the residence of Walter Pincus, and, as we waited for a response to Holmes's knock, Pincus strolled up the walk on his way home from work at a labouratory near the cathedral.

"What's this about?" he asked the three of us casually after we introduced ourselves, using our true identities.

"I would like to see an exemplar of your handwriting," Holmes said to shock him.

"I-I don't have any samples," Pincus stammered, turning rigid.

"Then have a seat at your table and take down my words on a sheet of foolscap," Holmes instructed. "Don't try to disguise your style, because I'll know if you do."

Red with anxiety, Pincus went to his bookshelf, grabbed some paper, withdrew a pencil from his kitchen cabinet, and sat.

"Dear Mr Latta," Holmes dictated. "I have never made your acquaintance, so allow me to introduce myself. I am an aquatic biologist and a botanist - "

"Alright! Alright!" Pincus yelled. "You have the goods on me! What becomes of me now?"

Special Constable Sidner placed him under arrest, and the four of us rode a Pullman car to New Alresford, while Pincus confessed. "Those conceited dry fly fishers treated us nymphers with disdain," he rambled with hostility, "and I was not about to tolerate their denying us our pleasures on the chalk streams."

Afterward, Holmes and I dined at Simpson's in the Strand, where he admitted he was embarrassed for having jumped to the conclusion that Professor Nicholls was the guilty one. "At times, Watson, the obvious solution to a problem is a deceiver. Do me a service, my good friend, if ever again I formulate a theory before all the data are in. Remind me of the day I went fishing for a killer and came away from his pond with my basket empty."

The End

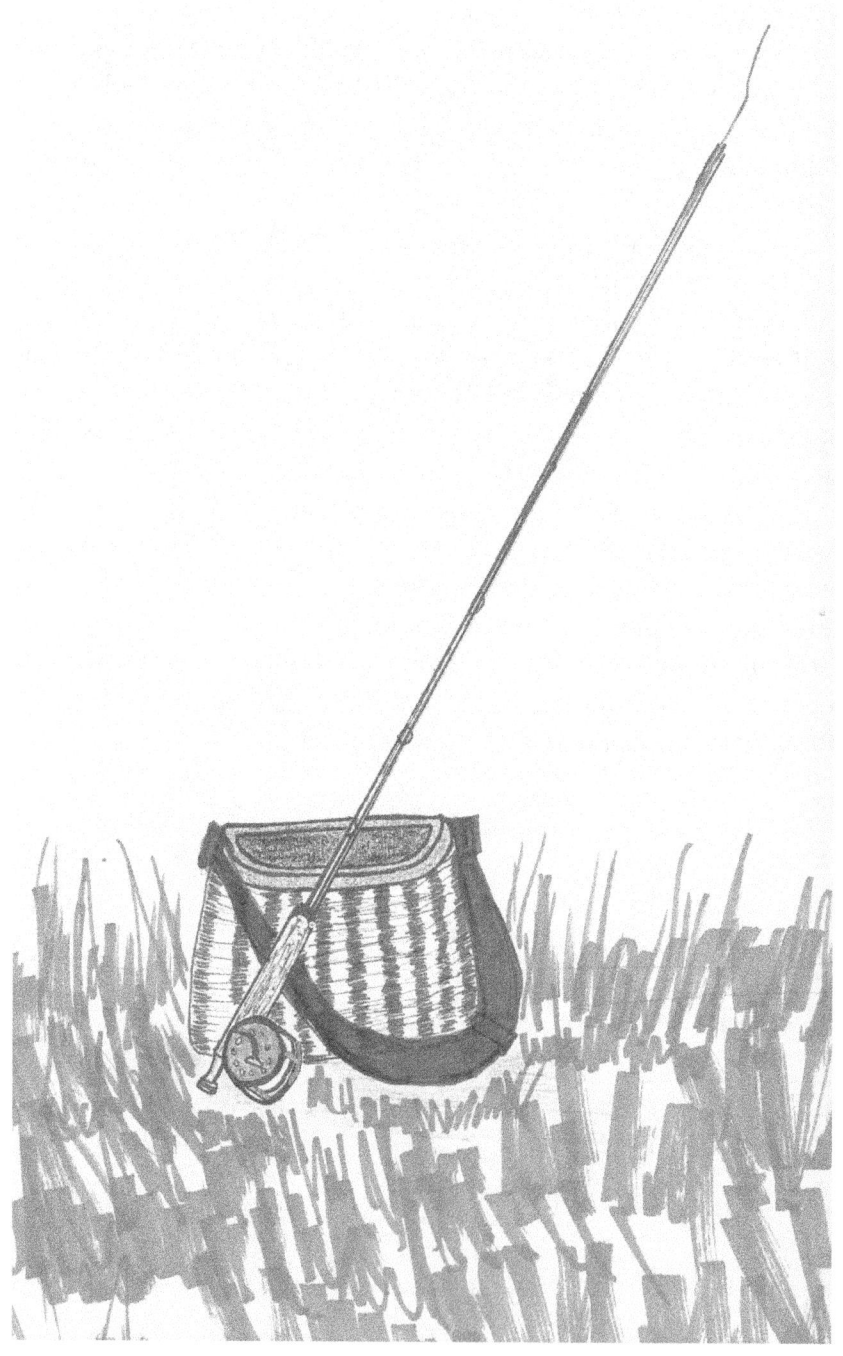

About the Author

Jack Grochot is a retired investigative newspaper journalist and a former federal law enforcement agent specializing in mail fraud cases. He lives on a small farm in southwestern Pennsylvania, where he writes and cares for five boarded horses. His fiction work has appeared in *Sherlock Holmes Mystery Magazine* and in an e-book anthology of Sherlock Holmes pastiches, both published by Wildside Press of Rockville, Maryland. Besides newspaper stories, Grochot has co-authored and edited a nonfiction book, *Pittsburgh Characters,* published by The Iconoclast Press of Greensburg, Pennsylvania. The author, an active member of Mystery Writers of America, can be contacted by e-mail: *grochot@comcast.net.*